LEGACY OF THE EASTER RISING:

BLOOD WILL HAVE BLOOD

LEGACY OF THE EASTER RISING:
BLOOD WILL HAVE BLOOD

JACK O'KEEFE, Ph.D.

CONTENTS

LEGACY OF THE EASTER RISING 1916

AUTHOR INFORMATION

JACK O'KEEFE, THE SON of Irish immigrants, earned a doctorate in English from Loyola University. After teaching at Power Memorial Academy in New York and Brother Rice High School in Chicago, he became a Professor of English for thirty-two years at Chicago City Colleges. Author of three books on the Irish—*Brother Sleeper Agent, Famine Ghost, and Survivors of the Great Irish Hunger*—O'Keefe lives with his wife in Chicago.

SUMMARY

THE BOOK BEGINS WITH a survey of the hatred between England and Ireland, dating back to the time of Queen Elizabeth, and then is followed by references to the Irish potato famine. American President Wilson was against Ireland in the Rising, even leaking information to the British.

This book reports on the turmoil of the 1916 Easter Rising in Dublin and focuses on an English killer, Major Browne, and an Irish soldier, Jerry Murphy. They encounter one another in Dingle where the Englishman murders the Irish rebel and sets in motion a trail of revenge.

After learning of his brother's death, Percival Browne begins his pursuit of Bart Murphy who has become a teaching Christian Brother. Murphy feels guilt over the shooting of the Englishman, and this follows him like a limpet all his life.

Murphy's superiors assign him to a Catholic school in New York with Browne still hunting him and taking a shot at him while he's on vacation. An Irish nurse cares for Murphy and is also attacked by Browne. Another Christian Brother wounds Browne. When the killer learns that Brother Murphy will go on a sabbatical to Dingle, he plans on shooting him there.

An FBI agent with an Irish background gets interested in the case and travels to Ireland to safeguard Murphy.

Keynote: This book begins with a description of the Easter Rising (1916) and then traces an English soldier's pursuit of his Irish enemy from Ireland to America and back.

Key words: Rising, Catholic, Michael Collins, Black and Tans, seminary, New York, Dublin, Hudson River, Roosevelt, Dingle, novitiate, cemetery

Excerpt: The most important event in Irish history, The Dublin Easter Rising of 1916, almost never came off. Michael Collins, later head of the Irish Free State, stated of the Rising, "On the whole it was bungled terribly, costing many a good life. It seemed at first to be well-organized, but afterward became subjected to panic decisions and to a great lack of essential organization and cooperation" (Coogan *1916* 126-127).

Many things went wrong before the Rising. Eoin MacNeill, head of the National Volunteers, a military organization with hundreds of members, opposed it, even writing in *The Irish Times* on Easter Sunday the day before the Rising that there should be no violence, causing confusion in its members—resulting in many men not partaking in the rebellion. A National Volunteer, Jerry Murphy, remained true to the Cause and wanted to fight.

"Blood will have blood, they say; blood will have blood" (*Macbeth*.3.4)

COVER

MARTYRS OF EASTER RISING 1916

Susan Clinard

1916 Easter Rising Memorial

From Susan Clinard
http://www.clinard.org/

THIS SCULPTURE IS THE work of Susan Clinard from Hamden, Conn., representing the faces of the signers of the Declaration of Irish Freedom in 1916—Thomas Clarke, Sean Mac Diermada, Thomas MacDonagh, P.H. Pearse, Eamonn Ceannt, James Connolly, and Joseph Plunkett. Affixed to the outside of the Gaelic American Club in Hamden, her piece reflects the energy of the leaders of the Easter Rising. For more of her work, consult her website at Susan@Clinard.org where she exhibits her art in wood, clay, wire, and mixed media. Having displayed her sculpture in Paris, Chicago, Yale University, and other venues, Susan Clinard is a working artist who has granted me permission to make her creation part of my book.

I am also grateful to Rich Powers, Chairperson of the 100th Anniversary of the Easter Rising Committee; Pat Dyer, Vice Chair; Tom Keane, Treasurer; and the following—Chris Conway, Dan Hines, Ted Lovely, and Pat O'Connell.

INTRODUCTION

THIS IS A HISTORICAL novel that explores the 1916 Easter Rising in Dublin and its consequences for an Irish Christian Brother. The chief source for the history of the Dublin events is Fearghal McGarry's *Easter Rising* (Oxford University 2010). Other sources include internet websites and personal records of the IRA for my father Denis O'Keefe, who killed an informer, O'Meara. I am also indebted to Steve Fitzgerald, Eric Brouwer and Alan Gbur for accounts of the Black and Tans and Irish soldiers, and to Brian Shanley for his encouragement.

Irish history is difficult to understand, much less write about, because one topic leads to another, opening up surprising avenues of thought and information. My parents and other Irish relatives called me a "narrowback" because unlike them, here in America, I didn't do physically demanding labor like work in the stockyards, or digging canals as they had. On a trip to Ireland, I was shocked when the natives didn't know the term or a similar one – "greenhorn" meaning rookie. As a youngster, I paid little attention to my family's folk history—which I deeply regret— but I also understood the Irish penchant for secrecy learned from a lifetime of living among informers and spies. In fact my father, Denis O'Keefe and a friend, formed part of a firing squad who executed an informer named O'Meara who was going to reveal to the Black and Tans the hiding place of Liam Lynch, IRA (Irish Republican Army) leader, local commander and Limerick.

The Easter Rising in 1916 wasn't the first sign of Irish revolt against the English. In New York, in 1916, German spies tried to blow up the Statue of Liberty. President Woodrow Wilson said he had no time to deal with a "regrettable incident at a private railroad terminal." The Irish Civil War with England started in Tom's River, New Jersey, very close to the Statue of Liberty. For years, America had been shipping guns and ammunition to the English. Germany spies using "pencil bombs" set fire to an ammunition dump on the night of July 30, 1916, causing more than one-hundred thousand dollars' worth of damage to Lady Liberty's torch, though fewer than ten people perished in the explosion. There is no evidence of Irish and American collaboration. It took fourteen years for Germany to reimburse America for the damages. Black Tom is not part of Liberty State Park. A small memorial features a circle of America flags and a plaque the describes the disaster and declares, "You are walking on a cite which saw one of the worse acts of terrorism in American History."

A HISTORY OF HATE

WHY DID THE IRISH hate the English? For 400 years since the time of Henry the VIII, Britain oppressed Ireland, chiefly because it was Catholic, not Church of England. In 1649-1650 at Drogheda, the Puritan Cromwell, who detested the Irish, slaughtered several thousand men, women, and children, even venturing to the Aran Islands 44 kilometers west of Galway to kill more Irish. Ironically, the English later beheaded Cromwell and buried him upside down.

In 1801 England bribed the Irish Parliament in the Act of Union to become part of the mother country. The Penal Laws soon followed, prohibiting the Irish from practicing their own faith and forbidding them to join any professions. Landlords, often absentee, evicted the natives from their land and sent farm produce to England making Ireland Britain's breadbasket. Christine Kinealy, a fellow at the University of Liverpool and the author of two scholarly texts on the Irish Famine: *This Great Calamity* and *A Death-Dealing Famine*, says that England shipped 9,992 calves from Ireland during "Black'47, " the worst Famine year, an increase of thirty-three percent from the previous year. In the twelve months following the second failure of the potato crop, England exported 4,000 horses and ponies. The transfer of livestock to Britain grew during the "Famine." In total, England appropriated over three million live animals from Ireland between 1846-1850, more than the number of people who emigrated during the famine years. Dr. Kinealy's most recent work is documented in the spring, 1998 issue of *History Ireland*. She states that almost 4,000 vessels carried food from Ireland to the ports of Bristol, Glasgow, Liverpool, and London during the worst year of the famine,

1847, when 400,000 Irish men, women, and children died of starvation and related diseases.

   Britain sent food under guard from the most famine-stricken parts of Ireland: Ballina, Ballyshannon, Bantry, Dingle, Killala, Kilrush, Limerick, Sligo, Tralee and Westport. During the Famine two million starving Irish died, and one million more fled the country in "coffin ships" overcrowded and filled with disease, conditions so bad that modern scholar Norita Fleming explains that "from Ireland to Grosse Ile in Canada, in the ocean graveyard, bodies could form a continuous chain of burial crosses" (O'Keefe *Famine Ghost* 11).

THE QUAKERS

THE QUAKERS WERE THE religious group most charitable to the Irish, providing them food, clothing, and equipment for the fisheries. "The Society of Friends did much to stay the plague and their work was carried on by volunteers who asked no reward. . . [The Quakers] spent no time in idle commenting on the Protestant or Papist faith, the Radical, Whig, or Tory politics, but looked at things as they were and faithfully recorded what they saw. . . they relieved, they talked and wrote, but acted more. As I followed in their wake through the country the name of 'blessed William Forster' was on the lips of the poor cabiners. . . When the question was put 'Who feeds you,' or 'Who sent you these clothes,' the answer was 'the good Quakers lady and they that have the religion entirely'" (Asenath Nicholson, [1792-1855] American philanthropist).

Quaker William Bennett, in charge of funding for the Irish poor, provides an eyewitness account of poverty in Mayo: "Upon entering a cabin in one corner there were three children huddled together scarcely visible from the smoke and rags covering them lying there because they were unable to rise, pale and ghastly . . . perfectly emaciated, voice gone, and evidently in the last stages of starvation" (Timothy Eagan, "Paul Ryan's Irish Amnesia," *New York Times* March 16, 2014).

Irish poverty and starvation was because of a character defect in the Irish charged, Charles Trevelyan, prime minister of England responsible for famine relief. In the Quinnipiac College Famine Museum hangs a picture of Trevelyan with the caption "For crimes against humanity, never brought to justice."

One million Irish died, one of every eight. Irish writer and polemicist John Mitchel charges "The Almighty sent the potato blight but the English created the famine" (Eagan).

An Irish Eviction

JOHN MITCHEL, LATER IMPRISONED for his views, went right to the heart of the matter: England's rulers described the famine as "a dispensation of Providence and ascribed it entirely to the blight of potatoes. But potatoes failed in like manner all over Europe, (yet only the Irish suffered its full effects) . . . . The Almighty indeed sent the potato blight, but the English created the famine" (*The History Place—Irish Potato Famine*).

English aristocrats appropriated Irish farms. In all, Kerry lost about 30% of its population to death and emigration, with an excess mortality rate of +15%. Most fled the country in the later decades of the nineteenth century and in the twentieth; Emigration from Kerry began on a large scale circa 1845, mainly to the east coast of the USA. People traveled to New York, Boston, Birmingham, and London. Deportation to Australia and Tasmania in 1840-1900 represent most of the resettlement there (rootsweb. ancestry.com/~irlker/famemig.html).

Besides taking their land and food, Britain also denied the Irish freedom to practice their religion until Daniel O'Connell and Catholic Emancipation Act in 1829. England allowed no school for Catholics, and children received no training in their faith except for so called "hedge schools" hidden in the rural areas. During this time the Irish prayed with the "penal rosary," a one-decade rosary because it was quicker than a full one recited in times of enforcement of the Penal Laws. By 1900 the Irish regained their land, but their resentment of England still festered. In the hearts and minds of the Irish, the accounts of English oppression were kept alive. When England refused to grant home rule to Ireland in 1913, hatred of England became stronger.

JERRY MURPHY

As Jerry Murphy began to head out east on the road in 1916 to Dublin, some two hundred miles through Cahirciveen and then to Tralee, he had two emotions, the excitement of going to fight for his country and the sadness of leaving his family. Sure they still hadn't recovered from the Famine of 1848. Even up here in the mountains, the ruins of tumbled cottages dotted the landscape. A million deaths— one of every eight Irishmen—starved because of English greed. His own people died of starvation and disease while the country's produce went to England by sea. He felt sorry for his parents but they could manage the farm and the few sheep on their own. He left the cottage just before dawn putting a letter explaining the reason for his behavior on the kitchen table for his parents.

He departed the house, stepping into the muddy road to begin his journey. He hoped that he might receive a ride from some farmer. There was no one about just a few sheep dogs from the Ahernes up the road. After walking for an hour, he saw someone ahead of him carrying a knapsack. It was a woman: what would she be doing on a lonely country road at this hour?

She was leading no cows or sheep. As he approached her, the sun came out, and he realized that he knew her, a pretty girl with ebony hair whom he had seen often at Mass at St. Mary's in Dingle. Not wishing to frighten her, he called out "Miss, can I walk with you? I mean you no harm. Oh I've seen you before — in town. Why are you out so early?"

Jerry Murphy and Bridie Kevane were the lone Dingle participants in the Easter Rising of 1916. Thomas Ashe was a good friend from the neighboring village of Lispole. Ashe's martyrdom spurred Murphy on, causing him to devote himself to the Irish cause. According to Jerry

Murphy, James Connolly and Patrick Pearse, the rebel leaders, erred in confining the rebellion to the poorer parts of Dublin, involving its residents in a battle that was not theirs to fight. "We need to strike at the heart of English power in the city," Jerry said, "not Monto and the other slums." The rebels bypassed the chance to take Dublin Castle, seat of English power in the city. Many "separation women" (so called because their spouses served in the British army in the Great War and were eligible for a death benefit should they die) opposed the Rising.

She said. "I know you from church. You're one of those boys sneaking a look at the girls when we're walking back from Communion."

Blushing, Jerry croaked "My name is Jerry Murphy, and you're Bridie Kevane one of the lads told me."

"So I am and I've noticed you sneaking looks at me."

Jerry answered, "I have, Bridie, why are you out so early?"

"To join my brother Eamon who's fighting the Brits."

"I'm doing the same. England has starved us. If it weren't for the priests and nuns, we wouldn't even have an education."

"We're of like mind," Bridie replied. "If we can walk to Tralee, I have an aunt and cousins there who will feed us."

As they were walking, they met a farmer with a wagonload of hay. "Sir, we're on our way to Tralee. Could we ride with you?"

"Certainly. I need the company. I'm Tom Linnane. Are ye two married?" "I see no rings." Blushing to the roots of her hair, Bridie replied "No."

"We 're going to Dublin to fight the Brits," answered Jerry.

"Ye have more courage than I do," Linnane answered.

After Mr. Linnane took them to Tralee, Bridie and Jerry resumed their trip to Dublin. They first reached Ashbourne, twenty miles outside Tralee, where they met Thomas Ashe, a farmer friend of Jerry's, a former teacher, who was leading the rebels. Ashe had captured and imprisoned thirty Brits in the local jail.

"Tom, this is my companion, Bridie Kavane, who wants to join the rebels."

"God bless. We can use you both at the GPO, our headquarters in Dublin."

"Is there work for a woman?" asked Bridie. "Yes, there are already over two hundred women working for the cause." Ashe's victory at Ashbourne became a model for future battles with his method of using the "flying column," which refers to the speed of movement of a group of rebels from place to place.

DUBLIN

As BRIDIE AND JERRY approached Dublin, the rattle of submachine guns made it clear that the battle was fierce. At the GPO, (General Post Office) center of the firing, the two met with Patrick Pearse, one of the leaders of the rising "We want to help," Jerry said. "Bridie, stand next to the wall behind me."

"We can use another rifle," Pearse replied. "And you young lady can help with the sick and wounded. One of our best men, James Connolly has a shattered ankle from an English sniper."

The GPO was a mess, rubble everywhere from the English 18 pounder cannons. Connolly had wrongly predicted the English would not use artillery in the city center, as Irish snipers were shooting from the open windows, with a half dozen wounded on the floor being helped by four women. These ladies had long helped the Irish cause for agrarian reform. Here they brought messages back and forth from the different strongholds.

Taught by Presentation nuns in Dingle, Bridie had some nursing experience. She helped James Connolly by cleaning and bandaging his ankle.

"Nurse, would you stay with me a while?" Connolly asked.

"Yes."

"My wife and family may come to see me, and I'd like to look as good as possible if the Brits come."

"Surely, Sir, there are nurses here that can tend the others. Heavy fighting is still going on around us. I'm not sure how long we can hold out."

After six days of heavy bombardment by English artillery, Patrick Pearse said, to Jerry and Bridie,"Enough of us will die here. You two should return to Dingle and spread the Cause. Sneak out the back way and leave."

During a lull in the battle, Pearse opened a back door for Bridie and Jerry who.

traveled the same road back to Dingle.

Upon reaching Dingle, in a meeting with the local rebels who were full of questions, Jerry said goodbye to Bridie and joined the rebels in Dingle.

Jerry Foy, a farmer from Lispole, asked about the Rising.

"Is it true women were allowed to fight with the rebels?"

"Yes, they were a great help to us."

President Wilson and the Easter Rising

No FRIEND OF THE Irish, President Wilson informed Britain of Germany shipping arms to Ireland.

In 1919 at the Paris Peace Conference American Wilson reneged on his promise to help Ireland achieve independence through his negotiations with England. Irish Americans wanted to keep the U.S. out of the war as an ally of England.

RISING

THE MOST IMPORTANT EVENT in Irish history, the Dublin Easter Rising of 1916, almost never came off. Michael Collins, later head of the Irish Free State, stated of the Rising, "On the whole it was bungled terribly, costing many a good life, but afterwards became subject to panic decisions and to a great lack of essential organization and cooperation" (Coogan *1916* 126-127).

Many things went wrong before the Rising began. Eoin MacNeill, head of the National Volunteers, a military organization with hundreds of members, opposed it, even writing in *The Irish Times* on Easter Sunday the day before the Rising that there should be peace, causing confusion in its members—resulting in many men not partaking in the rebellion.

One of MacNeill's motives for not rebelling was the capture of Roger Casement the day before and the scuttling of the German ship *Aud*, bringing arms and explosives Casement had negotiated for the Rising— a huge rebel loss.

As many as 135,000, of whom 35,000 died—feared they would lose their government pensions in a war with England—and attacked the rebels, as they had the prisoner Roger Casement in Tralee. Many of these women, especially from the slums, looted shops and stores giving the rebellion a bad name and frustrating its leaders: "Men, women, and even children seemed to have gone mad. In the cellars of one house in Henry Street, I saw them wading in wine over a foot deep" (Dennis Daly as quoted in McGarry 146). A Protestant clergyman wrote home: "The Dublin hooligans have come out of their holes like rats in a sewer. The slums of the north and south banks of the river have vomited their horrible brood" (McGarry 146).

One of the chief reasons for the Rising was the failure of England to pass a bill for Irish home rule though it was on the Parliament statute books—the British postponing its passage until after the Irish joined them in the Great War—-a quid pro quo. Yeats refers to this in his poem "Easter 1916," . . . "For England may yet keep faith/A terrible beauty is born." But Britain did not keep faith, resulting in the "terrible beauty" of the Rising.

ROGER CASEMENT: IRISH HERO

IN 1911 ENGLISH KING George V knighted Irishman Roger Casement for his charitable work in Africa, although Casement later became a leading Irish rebel, spending time in Germany negotiating the purchase of rifles, ammunition, and explosives for the rebels. Disappointed with the German failure to provide all the help he requested, Casement wished to call off the Rising. English soldiers arrested him in Tralee, and he was unable to contact rebel leaders. The Germans did send the *Aud,* with thousands of rifles and ammunition, but the British navy captured the ship and scuttled it outside Tralee.

Casement spent time in Germany with Plunkett negotiating the sale of arms for the Rising. Sailing off Tralee, Casement thought the Germans had betrayed him, and he wished like MacNeill, president of the National Volunteers, that the Irish would call off the revolt. Later Britain arrested him and sent him to Pentonville prison in England where the authorities executed him and threw his body into a grave filled with quicklime. Casement was homosexual giving Britain one more reason for executing him. Before his death Casement converted to Catholicism. Years later DeValera had his remains moved to Dublin where 500,000 people attended his wake and burial at Glasnevin Cemetery, resting place of many rebels.

Casement declared "Self-government is our right, a thing born in us at birth; a thing no more to be doled out to us or withheld from us by another people than the right to life itself" (***Wikipedia*** "Speech at the Dock").

Danger in Dublin

For days in 1916, rumors had floated in Dublin that some terrible event would arrive soon to shake Dublin. For years England had urged Irishmen to join their cause in the Great War, their "dual policy" extending the possibility that if the Irish cooperated with the Brits they might receive independence. The Irish were skeptical because Parliament had twice before vetoed granting Ireland freedom.

The Easter Rising in Dublin sparked an English overkill, the authorities executing fifteen of the rebels and shooting the wounded James Connolly after tying him to a chair. Typical of many Irish battles, hostilities broke out in confusion when the rifles and ammunition from Germany failed to arrive in Kerry.

One of the chief problems for the rebels was the opposition of Eoin McNeal of the National Volunteers who rushed to call off the rising, even placing an ad in the Sunday *Irish Times*. Only the hard-core rebels were determined to begin the rebellion at 11 o'clock on Easter Monday.

Why did the English react so slowly to the rebellion? The English government in Dublin knew nothing about the rebellion that was going to take place, while people on the fringes of society were aware of it. Jerry Murphy told Eoin MacNeill, "You're daft to call this off. The English are *eejits, amadans*." The historian Leon O'Broin asserts that "the British intelligence system in Ireland failed hopelessly" (McGarry 114). The Castle, the seat of English power in Dublin, had information, but failed to act upon it; for example, the British navy knew of the plans to land guns in Kerry but did not inform their leaders in Dublin. Much blame centers on Dublin Castle for their refusal to heed the many other warning signs; the lack of knowledge about the Rising caused a massive failure of intelligence.

Britain blamed long-serving chief secretary to Ireland Augustine Burrell for the failure, prompting him to resign a few weeks later. (irishcentral. com/roots/history/What-the-secret-police-files-on-the-1916-Rising-reveal. html)

THE RISING BEGINS

AT 11 O'CLOCK ON Easter Monday, 1916, the Rising began with the rebels seizing the General Post Office (GPO), Patrick Pearse reading a proclamation before a small crowd declaring Ireland's independence from Britain. The rebels printed Pearse's document which schools later taught and which became a rallying cry for years:

POBLACHT NA h-EIREANN
THE PROVISIONAL GOVERNMENT OF THE
IRISH REPUBLIC
TO THE PEOPLE OF IRELAND
IRISHMEN AND IRISHWOMEN: In the name of God and of the dead generations from which she receives her old tradition of nationhood, Ireland, through us, summons her children to her flag and strikes for her freedom.

Having organized and trained her manhood through her secret revolutionary organization, the Irish Republican Brotherhood, and through her open military organizations, the Irish Volunteers and the Irish Citizen Army, having patiently perfected her discipline, having resolutely waited for the right moment to reveal itself, she now seizes that moment, and supported by her exiled children in America and by gallant allies in Europe, but relying in the first on her own strength, she strikes in full confidence of victory.

We declare the right of the people of Ireland to the ownership of Ireland, and to the unfettered control of Irish destinies, to be sovereign and indefeasible.

The long usurpation of that right by a foreign people and government has not extinguished the right, nor can it ever be extinguished except by the destruction of the Irish people. In every generation the Irish people have asserted their right to national freedom and sovereignty; six times during the past three hundred years they have asserted it in arms. Standing on that fundamental right and again asserting it in arms in the face of the world, we hereby proclaim the Irish Republic as a Sovereign Independent State. And we pledge our lives and the lives of our comrades-in-arms to the cause of its freedom, of its welfare, and of its exaltation among the nations.

The Irish Republic is entitled to, and hereby claims, the allegiance of every Irishman and Irish woman. The Republic guarantees religious and civil liberty, equal rights and equal opportunities of all its citizens, and declares its resolve to pursue the happiness and prosperity of the whole nation and of all its parts, cherishing all the children of the nation equally, and oblivious of the differences carefully fostered by an alien government, which have divided a minority in the past.

Until our arms have brought the opportune moment for the establishment of a permanent National Government, representative of the whole people of Ireland and elected by the suffrages of all her men and women, the Provisional Government, hereby constituted, will administer the civil and military affairs of the Republic in trust for the people.

We place the cause of the Irish Republic under the protection of the Most High God, Whose blessing we invoke upon our arms, and we pray that no one who serves that cause will dishonour it by cowardice, inhumanity, or rapine. In this supreme hour, the Irish nation must, by its valour and discipline and by the readiness of its children to sacrifice themselves for the common good, prove itself worthy of the august destiny to which it is called.

Signed on behalf of the Provisional Government,

THOMAS J. CLARKE
SEAN MAC DIERMADA THOMAS MACDONAGH
P.H.PEARSE EAMONN CEANNT
JAMES CONNOLLY JOSEPH PLUNKETT

AT THE GPO (GENERAL POST OFFICE)

JERRY MURPHY, THE DINGLE volunteer, stood by an open window in the GPO when a wounded English soldier fell just outside, but within shooting range. One rebel said, "Jerry, shoot the bastard." Patrick Pearse, however, rebuked the man: "No useless outpouring of blood." Murphy complied and under a white flag of truce was dragging the wounded man to safety when out of the corner of his eye he saw a British officer in a crowd of others aiming at soldier: "I'm taking this man to your own lines," Murphy yelled. "Don't shoot."

"I don't care," Major Browne yelled. "I'm going to finish you off now. That will make one fewer of you to shoot later." Browne fired at Jerry, but the bullet thudded into the soldier he was carrying.

"You bastard," Jerry yelled. "You've hit one of your own. I'll get you some day." Browne's last shot hit the oak door of the GPO as one of the other rebels slammed it shut.

———❖———

On Tuesday of the week of the Rising, Lord Lieutenant Viscount Winborne imposed a curfew from 7 p.m. to 5:30 a.m., the next day expanding it to the whole nation, making life more difficult for citizens. Armed British snipers mounted on rooftops increased the danger. Dubliners had to navigate through the destruction of large buildings in the streets caused by heavy shelling. On Wednesday the English attacked in force. When fire swept the GPO on the weekend, the battle was over. The British rounded up over 2000 prisoners and crammed them into cattle boats for the trip to the internment camps in England.

Like many rebels in the Rising, Jerry Murphy desired death rather than surrender, but Patrick Pearse convinced him to return to Dingle to work for the Cause rather than die: "Sure, Jerry, enough of us will die here. We need you to spread our cause into the west of Ireland."

Having escaped arrest through a window at the back of the GPO, Jerry Murphy and Bridie Kevane passed through Banna Strand in Tralee where only a few days before the English had captured Irishman Roger Casement.

Martyrs

The spiritual effects of the Rising revealed themselves quickly in the number of Requiem Masses for those executed because the identification of the rebellion with Christ's suffering and death resonated with the Irish people. Catholics printed thousands of holy cards with pictures of martyred rebels.

KILMAINHAM JAIL

Kilmainham Jail was the most infamous prison in Ireland. After the rebels surrendered, it was here that the British interned them. Built in 1796, the place was dark and cold, candles supplying the only heat. It hadn't been used for sixteen years. It had iron bars throughout and a set of steep stairs ascending to the second and third floors. Each cell was two square meters shackling, not only the prisoners but their spirits too (ireland-information. com/irishholidays-irishtourist/kilmainham-gaol-dublin.htm).

From May 3rd to May 9, 1916, the English executed fifteen of the rebels, all signers of Pearse's Proclamation.

Anxious to kill more Irish like those who had caused him his lost ear at the Somme, Major Browne took charge of the execution squad. The last victim was James Connolly one of the Rising leaders. Unable to stand because of a shattered ankle from a bullet wound, Browne shouted, "We'll get you anyway." Browne ordered one of his men Sergeant Ryan, to get a chair and some rope to tie him down.

A Capuchin priest stood next to Connolly praying. "I'd like to kill you too," Browne screamed, "despite the dog collar you're wearing." Then one of the soldiers pinned a white piece of paper over Connolly's heart. Browne fired the first shot from his rifle followed by the other soldiers, and the martyr fell dead.

"Take the body and dump it with the others into the lorry, so we can cart them off for burial," Browne ordered. When word leaked out that Browne was the executioner, Jerry Murphy said, "He's the same bastard who killed one of his own at the GPO."

Prison cell in Kilmainham

From Pixabay free copyright
https://pixabay.com/en/prison-ruin-cell-bed-toilet-jail-451442/

Capuchin priests heard Confession and accompanied the prisoners until the moment of their death in stonebreakers' yard. Patrick Pearse told Murphy "These Capuchin priests, good men and brave, hear our Confessions. They'll hear yours too."

"Yes," Murphy said, "You never know how we'll end up here."

To protect women prisoners from harassment by English guards, Capuchin friars stayed the night in Kilmainham. The women suffered many indignities, like not being able to relieve themselves or having to use a closet for a lavatory. Food was sparse, and the prisoners received no exercise.

In Charge

On Friday the week of the Rising, the English appointed Major General John Maxwell, who had been serving in Egypt, commander of the British troops in Ireland. Maxwell blamed the Rising on priests and radical women, some 200 of them, involved in the rebellion. His blaming priests was patently wrong, the Catholic hierarchy against the rebellion — while local priests supported it.

Conditions in Kilmainham Jail were terrible: cold, darkness, and torture by guards. The executions of the prisoners were secret. The English took them into a small courtyard where soldiers blindfolded them, placed a small paper over their hearts, forced them to sit on wooden crates, and shot them in the early hours of the morning.

Stonebreaker's Yard, location of the bodies of the Irish martyrs.

From the National Inventory of Architectural Heritage

http://www.buildingsofireland.ie/Surveys/Buildings/ BuildingoftheMonth/Archive/Name,3083,en.html

Arthur Griffith, later founder of Sinn Fein (Ourselves Alone) and negotiator with Collins of the Peace Treaty, stated "Something of the primitive awoke in me. I clenched my fists with of rage and I longed for vengeance" (McGarry 280). Irish playwright and author George Bernard Shaw opposed the shooting of the Irish rebels: "My own view is that the men who were shot, in cold blood, after their capture or surrender, were prisoners of war and it was entirely incorrect to slaughter them . . . The military authorities in the English government must have known that they were canonizing their prisoners. . ." (Coogan, *Michael Collins*). Of those who were against the rebellion, Pearse stated "People will say hard things about us now, but we shall be remembered by posterity and blessed by the future" (McGarry 197).

In his final words, fellow martyr James Connolly stated his reasoning for the Rising: "We went out to break the connection between this country and the British Empire, and to establish an Irish Republic . . . We succeeded in proving that Irishmen are ready to die . . . As long as that remains the case, the cause for Irish freedom is safe. Believing that the British Government has no right in Ireland ... makes that Government forever a usurpation and a crime against human progress. I personally thank God that I have lived to see the day when thousands of Irish men and boys, and hundreds of Irish women and girls, were ready to affirm that truth, and to attest it with their lives if need be" (hallamor.org/1916-series-easter-rising-executions-final-day). It was the timing and the manner of the executions that so shocked and enraged the Irish.

GREAT WAR

IRISH SOLDIERS IN ENGLAND

AT THE SAME TIME as the Rising, 135,000 Irishmen were fighting for the British army in France, 35,000 of whom would die there. When word about the killing of the martyrs reached them, their morale suffered and their effectiveness as fighters lessened. The shootings affected Irish elsewhere, especially in the United States. The British carried the killings out from May 3 through 1916, May 12, — 100 years ago, — with a few hours' notice to each condemned man, after secret summary courts martial. The Irish public could hear the volleys of the firing squads, but the English announced the executions publicly only after the men were dead.

When news of the executions of the rebels reached the soldiers fighting the Germans, the morale of the Irish soldiers dipped considerably. Here were the Irish soldiers fighting for the country which was murdering their own people at home.

PRISON CAMP

ALONG WITH HUNDREDS OF others, the British sent Michael Collins to an internment camp, Frongoch in Wales. The prisoners formed bonds and reinforced their beliefs, becoming the nucleus of the troops for the War of Independence. During this time, Collins was communicating with Thomas Ashe just months before the young man's death.

When Britain wanted America to join the Great War, she tried to curry favor by releasing the inmates in December of 1916.

Ironically, the British assembled the best of a generation of radicals and allowed them, in the camp at Frongoch, to plan the strategy of the future, especially the civil war.

Conditions at Frongoch were never easy. The old buildings were bitterly cold at night, very hot during the day, an infestation by rats plagued the prisoners.

While the presence of Irish dissidents was well known locally — although the camp was guarded by soldiers, many locals worked there, in the kitchens and barrack blocks, and came into regular contact with the Irishmen — The British Government warned the press to be careful about what they published about the location of the camp (*dailypost*.co.uk/news/local-news/ww1-prisoner-war-camp-bala).

HARSHNESS OF TREATMENT OF THE REBELS

JOHN DILLON, AN M.P. for 35 years, said of the English suppression of the Rising: "in the whole of modern history . . . there has no rebellion or insurrection put down with so much blood and so much savagery. . ." (McGarry 185). According to a Kerry volunteer, many separatists viewed the execution of the martyrs "as the tipping point for broader nationalist opinion; the people who before took the Volunteers with a smile changed completely. A new Ireland has been born" (McGarry 280). The killing of the martyrs transformed the views of the Irish people about them. They became heroes.

Pope Benedict supported the rebellion. In the minds of many who took part in the Rising, the fight was for faith as well as fatherland. The rebels sent papal count George Plunkett to Rome a fortnight before the Rising to seek the blessing of Benedict XV on the revolt (*irishtimes.com/* opinion/eamonn-mccann-role-of-catholic-church-in-easter-rising-should-be-remembered).

Despite pressure from Irish Americans to not execute the rebels, thinking England wanted help in the Great War and would release them, only DeValera and Countess Markiewicz avoided the death penalty.

Two years later in 1918 when Britain wished to begin conscription, Irish bishops opposed the idea and at the Maynooth Conference instructed their parishioners, to sign a pledge "Denying the right of the British government to enforce compulsory service in this country, we pledge ourselves solemnly to one another to resist conscription by the most effective means at our disposal" (wikipedia.org/wiki/Conscription_Crisis_of_1918).

Search for Irish Volunteers for England in WWI

From the Library of Congress
http://www.loc.gov/pictures/item/2003668492/

With Ireland being so Catholic (more than half the rebels were from schools of the Christian Brothers, like Jerry Murphy), it is no surprise that almost all the rebels were of the same faith. English commander General Maxwell heaped one final indignity on them when he had them interred in non-consecrated ground with no priest officiating. Count Plunkett had visited the Vatican and told the Pope the rebels wished to die as Catholics. Catholic clergy served an important role in the Rising: mediating between soldiers to lessen the violence, procuring medical help, and counseling the sick and dying.

The one constant in the Irish struggles with England was Winston Churchill who along with Lloyd George convinced Michael Collins to sign the peace treaty that led to his death. He also masterminded the forming of the Black and Tans in 1920 and let them loose on Ireland. A bloody civil war, the pro-union force under de Valera and the Free State under the leadership of Michael Collins.

Back in Dingle, after the fighting in Dublin, Jerry Murphy explained to his men that the British even killed children in the Rising, for example, fifteen-year-old Charles D'Arcy. He and 39 other children, including a two-year-old in a baby carriage died (historyireland. com/20th-century-contemporary-history/children-of-the-revolution/).

Bombardment from shelling caused fires that ended the Rising, the Crown troops destroying any building that might house rebels.

INFORMATION ABOUT MARTYRS

ALTHOUGH THERE WERE NO copies of remarks made by the martyrs from their court appearances, some of the trials provided a forum for them. One of the most powerful was from Patrick Pearse: "When I was a child of ten I went down by my bedside and promised God that I should devote my life to an effort to free my country. . . If you strike us down now we shall rise again and renew the fight. You cannot reconquer Ireland. You cannot extinguish the Irish passion for freedom. If one deed has not been sufficient to win freedom, then our children will win it by a better deed" (McGarry 271). Pearse so impressed the judge, Brigadier General Blackader, that he regretted "having to condemn to death one of the finest characters I have ever come across. There must be something very wrong in the state of things that makes a man like that become a rebel" (McGarry 271).

Prime Minister Asquith speaking to Parliament praised the rebels: "So far as the great body of insurgents is concerned, I have no hesitation saying that they have conducted themselves with great humanity which contrasted very much to their advantage with the so-called civilized enemies in Europe. . . They fought very bravely and did not resort to outrage" (Coogan 146).

Some newspapers, however, were scornful of the rebel leaders: "Pearse was a man of ill-balanced mind, if not actually insane . . . selecting him as 'chief magistrate' was enough to create doubts about the sanity of those who approved . . . no reason to lament that its perpetrators have met the fate universally reserved for traitors . . . (*The Irish Catholic*, May 29, 1916).

The Irish resented how uneven the sentences were; for example, Thomas Ashe and Richard Mulcahy, leaders of the victory at Ashbourne, received no sentence of death, but Willie Pearse did—because he was the brother of Patrick Pearse.

"The only good thing about the trials was they didn't execute my neighbor Thomas Ashe," explained Jerry Murphy. But then Ashe would die of force-feeding the following year.

When the English marched prisoners from their garrisons to Kilmainham after the Rising, some citizens threw garbage or the contents of chamber pots at the captured rebels. Despite their poor treatment by Dubliners and the press, the prisoners were still defiant—singing Irish gallows songs.

All in all, the Rising claimed 1350 deaths with 61000 yards of buildings destroyed at a cost of 2,250,000 pounds.

Stationed in the GPO, Jerry Murphy followed reports of the cruelty of Major Reginald Browne toward civilians; for example, Browne shot and killed well-known pacifist Francis Sheehy-Skeffingon.

Not all the losses were rebels. The British suffered 116 dead, 368 wounded, and nine missing. 16 policemen died, and 29 were wounded. The rebels suffered 64 casualties 2,127 wounded, including civilians (en. wikipedia.org/wiki/Grangegorman_Military_Cemetery). Artillery fire caused the deaths of most civilians. The rebels had no artillery, only rifles.

The Volunteers and ICA (Irish Civilian Army) recorded 64 killed in action, but otherwise Irish casualties were not divided into rebels and civilians. All 16 police fatalities and 22 of the British soldiers killed were Irishmen. British families came to Dublin Castle in May 1916 to reclaim the bodies and to arrange funerals. The British shot citizens deliberately on occasion when they refused to obey orders such as to stop at checkpoints. On top of that, there were two instances of British troops murdering civilians out of revenge or frustration, at Portobello Barracks, where six died, and North King Street, where they killed fifteen.

Indirect fire from artillery, heavy machine guns and incendiary shells killed the majority of civilians. The British, who used such weapons extensively, caused most non-combatant deaths (belfasttelegraph.co.uk/news/republic-of-ireland/ireland-commemorates-children-killed-in-easter-rising-lets-build-a-republic-they-would-be-proud-of-says-president-higgins).

Important buildings fell victim to destruction, for example, Clery's Department Store and the Imperial Hotel as well as the GPO.

————◇◆◇◆◇————

A series of courts martial beginning on 2 May, sentenced 90 people to death (historyireland.com/20th-century-contemporary-history/children-of-the-revolution). General Maxwell, English commander, confirmed 15 of them (including all seven signatories of the Proclamation). Capt. HV Stanley explained: "I was the Medical Officer who attended the executions of the first nine *Sinn Féiners*, (Ourselves Alone) to be shot. After that I got so sick of the slaughter that I asked to be changed. Three refused to have their eyes bandaged. The rifles of the firing party were waving like a field of corn. All the men were cut to ribbons at a range of about 10 yards" (index. php/rising/aftermath/).

Conditions in Kilmainham were terrible for the rebels: little water or food and no privacy. Not all the victims were leaders: From the outset, Maxwell was determined that he would not release the bodies of the executed men to their families, fearing that "Irish sentimentality will turn those graves into martyrs' shrines to which annual processions etc. will be made. [Hence] the executed rebels are to be buried in quicklime, without coffins" (*Easter Rising*, Foy and Barton 307).

Jerry Murphy learned from a police officer friend that the English buried the bodies of the executed 1916 leaders in a pit of quicklime, and some DMP (Dublin Metropolitan Police) reported that they were buried in the order in which they died.

Behind the pit where there is a wall with the Proclamation of the Irish Republic in Irish and English. No epitaph memorializes the men buried there, only their names in the concrete wall surrounding the grave in Arbour Hill, unmarked and identifiable only by its proximity to the wall and the flagpoles there. There is no eternal flame, and no individual tributes to the executed men.

The graves are under a low mound on a terrace of Wicklow granite in what was once the old prison yard.

Each of the men's families had requested that their executed bodies be released to them, but General Maxwell decided not to grant their wishes.

The majority of the men executed for their part in the Easter insurrection were deeply committed Catholics – even the socialist Connolly received Communion from Capuchin Fr Aloysius – and there is no doubt that their Catholic faith meant a great deal to the executed men.

In a final insult to their leadership, the English buried them in unconsecrated ground (Joe Connell youtube.com/watch?v=ZahnmJoalDM).

Eventually, word seeped out about the rebels executed in Dublin, but the English released no information from the trials, fearing those accounts would only stir up more hatred.

Almost all the rebels were Catholic and believed in Pearse's idea of a blood sacrifice:

"What did they do, Oh Irishmen whose souls are dead. . .

And walked the way saints have led

You ask of me what did they do who have led

I ask of you—what did Christ do?"

(as quoted in Joost Augustin *The Irish Revolution 1913-1923*).

Some of the survivors of the Rising went on to become leaders of the independent Irish state like Collins and Griffith.

By drawing a large number of people into political activism, the issue of the prisoners provided a strong connection between the rebels and the more organized Sinn Fein. The rebels joined "the pantheon of martyrs who had devoted themselves all to the same cause. Surely it is the most glorious cause in history" (Casement quoted in McGarry 275).

ANALYSIS OF THE HISTORY OF THE RISING

HISTORIAN ROY FOSTER ASSERTS that the Rising was indeed the 'blood sacrifice' that Patrick Pearse insisted was necessary for new Ireland's birth. "what shines through many of the voices of those who lived through this era is the integrity and idealism of a generation of Irish men and women who struggled to realize a vision of an Ireland different to the one in which they had been born" (McGarry 293) (socialistreview.org.uk/304/ rising-and-revisionism).

REGINALD BROWNE – A BAD MAN

LONDON-BORN REGINALD BROWNE SERVED in the Great War for England. At the battle of the Somme in France, a captain demanded he rescue three Irish soldiers caught between the lines in "no man's land." After creeping under the barbed wire, Browne screamed at the soldiers, "You dumb bastards, crawl back to our own men." Then a German grenade exploded against the right side of his face destroying his right ear. A field doctor operated on him and grafted skin from his leg to close the wound leaving that side of his face pink and shiny. Though the doctor saved his life, Brown always hated the Irish who led him into danger. As he walked or stood, he listed to the left side to hear better. When the Easter Rising broke out, the army sent him to Dublin, first promoting him to major despite the loss of his ear.

On Easter Wednesday in Dublin, Browne was part of the first group of soldiers mauled by the Irish in front of the G.P.O. Forced by their commanders to charge again the next day, Browne confronted an Irish resident in the street who said: "Officer, please don't shoot. I'm not a soldier and have no weapon."

Browne retorted, "If you're that dumb, you deserve to die." Browne shot the man dead with his Webley revolver.

When the English executed all the signers of the Freedom Proclamation, Browne volunteered for the firing squad that shot the martyrs, saying "I'd just as soon shoot them, as look at them." They took my ear at Somme.

AFTERMATH

Two years after the Rising, in 1918, Churchill formed a small army of 9,500 Black and Tans (so named because their uniforms were khaki and black). Most of them had served in the British army and needed work after the war, serving in Ireland in 1920–1922. More than one-third of them died or left the service before they were disbanded along with the rest of the Royal Irish Constabulary in 1922, an extremely high wastage rate, and well over half received government pensions. A total of 404 members of the RIC died in the conflict with more than 600 were wounded (*Wikipedia*, the free encyclopedia).

The Black and Tans committed many atrocities, perhaps the worst the random killing of thirteen citizens including two children at Croke Park in Dublin at a football game. One of those in attendance that day was Jim Fitzgerald who disappeared for two years after the massacre. The Tans terrorized small towns too, imposing curfews. The army veterans had some discipline, but others among them were lawless thugs released from jail. In the village of Hospital near Limerick, Tans killed a teenage boy out saying his rosary during curfew. A statue memorializing his death still remains there. In another incident two young men, Denis O'Keefe and Jack Kiefe, killed an informer named O'Meara, a former British soldier expelled for drunkenness. He had threatened to reveal to the Tans the location of Liam Lynch, a local leader. O'Keefe left the country for the U.S. where he got a job in the stockyards in Chicago.

MURPHY RETURNS HOME

JERRY'S ROUTE TO DINGLE was over Connor Pass, more dangerous but less traveled than the flatter road through Anascaul that paralleled the ocean.

As he walked over the mountains, Jerry could not help but think how beautiful this country was, only to be scarred by war. He realized too that the enemy wouldn't confine themselves only to Dublin. When Jerry reached Dingle, he met with his five rebel friends: Art Shires, Jim Snyder, John Glennon, Peter Doyle, and John Coleman. Gathering in the Gallarus Oratory, a medieval church, a hundred-year-old beehive stone hut four miles west of Dingle.

Jerry told them about the murder of Francis Sheehy-Skeffington, a prominent pacifist, killed without trial. "Sure he wasn't even a rebel."

Assembled with his men, Jerry said, "Now boys, what's the first thing we should do?"

"Get the damn Tans out of Dingle," Art Shires said.

"Fair enough," Jerry said. "The best time is 7:00 just before curfew."

On a Friday the Tans left their Dingle barracks and headed up the mountain toward Mt. Brandon where Jerry's own family lived in a one-story house. His parents, Dan and Mary Murphy and his younger brother Bart were relieved to see him safe after the Rising, young Bart peppering him with questions—how many were killed? Did he know Patrick Pearse, James Connolly, or any of the other heroes of the Rebellion?

Jerry replied, "I knew them all. James Connolly suffered a terrible wound to his ankle crippling him so he couldn't stand, so the Brits tied him to a chair to shoot him."

Seamus Murdoch explained, "The Tans here in town have a new leader, a Major Browne, wounded in the Great War. He was in charge of the siege of Tralee when the English shot and killed ten people coming from Mass on All Saints' Day. He then had his men destroy the creamery, depriving the people of food and jobs."

"Browne, that was the bastard in Dublin who shot one of his own men. He badly needs killing," Jerry Murphy said. "We'll do for him here."

Major Browne learned that Jerry Murphy, a Dingle man, had partaken in the Easter Rising, the only Dingle man to do so along with Bridie Kevane. Browne said to his men, "We missed him in Dublin, but not here."

A week later a gray Tan lorry trundled into Dingle. The Tans chose as their barracks, a squat stone building of two floors with four windows in front reinforced by wooden barricades. Standing on Main Street, cottages of residents surrounded the building. A short distance away, the Church of the Sacred Heart loomed alongside the Christian Brothers school. Once he had reconnoitered the area, Major Browne told his men "Board up the windows because I don't want the rebels seeing what we are up to." For meals the major recruited a woman, Fiona Sheehy, a widow who ran a boarding house down the street and prepared dinner promptly at 1:00 p.m. each day for him and his four soldiers. "Tell the woman to have no truck with the rebels," he said. "We don't need poisoning." A good cook, Mrs. Sheehy often made lamb stew or cod with potatoes and dulse, a vegetable from the seashore.

The major imposed a dusk to dawn curfew. With only one ear, Browne was conspicuous during the day on the street, usually leaving the barracks only at night to walk his bulldog Winston who had a personality like his master—mean. The neighbors kept close watch on the troops. Jerry Murphy and his men moved out of the Gallarus Oratory to a farmhouse just north and west of town abandoned since the time of the Famine. Jerry designated Dan Waddick as lookout to watch for any Black and Tan movement. From the Tralee IRA, Jerry received six Enfield rifles and ammunition, hauled across Connor Pass by Jim Stack, giving his group enough firepower to attack the Tans in Dingle.

On some days Browne led his troops on sorties to Lispole, Ballyferriter and Ventry to search for any rebels, but they had little success. When he saw the Tans leaving Dingle, Seamus Murdoch would light a fire of peat and wood in the fields behind his house as a warning that the Brits were on the move.

Jerry Murphy said to his men "We'll hit the Tans when they're out of town away from the safety of their barracks. If we could pick off one or two it would be a blessing for us." His men agreed. Murphy knew it was important to keep his men sharp for fighting.

Trouble came to the rebels from surprising sources. The Dingle soldiers had an informer, possibly a woman. Some of the IRA suspected Mary Manning, the younger sister of their cook, Fiona Sheehy. Mary helped her sister prepare dinner every day and caught a bit of gossip from the troops. Also, without her sister's knowledge, Mary became a mistress of Major Browne. As a suitor he was totally wrapped up in himself, caring nothing about Mary's pleasures as long as he had his. Browne paid her a few pounds every week.

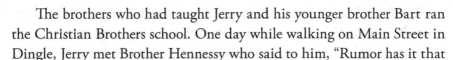

The brothers who had taught Jerry and his younger brother Bart ran the Christian Brothers school. One day while walking on Main Street in Dingle, Jerry met Brother Hennessy who said to him, "Rumor has it that you're leading the rebels here in town."

"Yes, Brother."

"Be careful then. These fellas have no mercy."

"I know, Brother. I saw their work in the Easter Rising."

"Yes, Jerry. Seven of the fourteen martyrs were from brothers' schools. I taught Tom Clarke in Limerick."

"Brother, I have the sense that an informer is reporting on us."

"We hear rumors about the women cooking for the Tans, not the older one but the younger one Fiona."

Just to check further, Jerry went to Dingle town to with his Dublin companion Bridie Kevane, who knew everyone in town. "Bridie, we think there is an informer reporting on us."

"You men, you don't see what is staring you in the face. The young girl Fiona. Sure, she'd lie with a dog."

Jerry accosted Fiona one night after the Tan dinner. "We hear you're feeding information about us to the Tans."

"What would you have me do, a poor widow? He gives me five pounds for sharing his bed, God forgive me. He will if you do this no more."

"Fiona, if you inform on us again, you're a dead woman."

After Browne shot his brother Jerry, Bart Murphy was torn. Christ had forgiven His enemies. He was God. Bart wasn't.

Bridie Kevane heard the news of Jerry's death, but she wanted to see for herself. When she met Bart stumbling and crying on the road, she knew the story was true. "I loved him. Where is he now?' She went to the body with Bart clasping lover. Bart said "Clear out, Bridie. They may shoot you too."

Bart burned for revenge. Even though Jerry had been in the Rising, he had killed no one, even dragging a Brit to safety from the GPO.

Another side of Bart was that he wanted to become a Christian brother, the order founded by Edmund Rice to teach poor boys, sending his men to America and Canada to teach in inner cities. They had taught him in Dingle. Teaching the poor appealed to his imagination, but first he had to reconcile his wish for revenge. The only person that knew about his conflicted feelings was Seamus Murdoch whom Bart wished to recruit to kill Major Browne. In addition to killing Jerry, Browne had shot Father Griffin in Galway and murdered men coming from Mass in Tralee where he also destroyed the local creamery, depriving the residents of jobs and food. He was a bad man, but Bart knew the Sixth Commandment "Thou shalt not kill." Somehow he had to reconcile his hatred for Browne with the Commandment.

Bloody Sunday

After the murders of Jerry Murphy and Father Griffin, and the siege of Tralee, violence burst in Dublin master-minded by Michael Collins.

With help from his spies in British headquarters in Dublin Castle on *December* 21, 1920, IRA men shot and killed twelve English spies.

That same afternoon the English went to Croke Park in Dublin where Dublin and Tipperary were playing a football match. On the pretext that they were searching for weapons, the English raked the crowd with rifles and automatic weapons resulting in fourteen civilian deaths including two small boys. Fourteen British were killed. Despite the Irish losses, the battle was hailed as a victory for the IRA because publication of the Croke Park massacre brought attention to the Irish cause all over the world.

One eyewitness to the slaughter was Jim "The Bruiser" Fitzgerald who went into hiding for two years after the incident. Not until after his death did a local radio station broadcast in Gaelic an interview he had given years before with the guerilla mentality "you just don't tell what you did with whom" (*The World of Hibernia* Summer 1997).

Michael Collins had planned the murder of English spies called the Cairo gang that Sunday morning. For revenge against the Irish, the English used submachine guns.

TRIP TO BALDOYLE

THE BROTHERS IN DINGLE approved Bart's application to become a Christian brother despite his borrowing a gun from them, so he and his father borrowed a horse and trap for the journey of four hours to Dublin and the seminary. They had reached West Cork near Kilmichael when Bart said, "Da, pull off to the side; there's shooting here." An IRA leader told Bart and his father to take a parallel road through West Cork. A squadron of thirty-six IRA men lay prone on both sides of the Macroom road near Kilmichael and ambushed two Tan lorries.

Led by Tom Barry, the IRA killed sixteen men with two of their own critically injured. This shooting occurred in the days following Bloody Sunday in Dublin and marked an escalation in the Anglo-Irish war.

As they drove off, the father and son both remarked that violence had become an increased part of life in Ireland.

Just as they passed the ambush site at Kilmichael, Bart and his father met a caravan of tinkers coming towards them, six people riding in a cart pulled by a black and white pony. "Da, get off the road so these tinkers can go through."

"Right you are, Bart. They're a tough looking crowd. They're speaking in cant or *shelta,* their own language. You can 't trust them; sure, they'd steal the eye out of your head."

"Not many of them around us at home, probably because we're so far from big towns.”

Visit from the Big Fella

As Bart was ending his first year as a novice, a Crossley Tender drove up the driveway to Baldoyle. Out stepped Michael Collins with two other IRA men carrying weapons. They were carrying Thompson submachine guns smuggled in automobiles from America through Liverpool. In a phone call, they had asked Brother Chapman if they could hold shooting practice in the woods at the rear of Baldoyle. Br. Chapman agreed. The three IRA men walked to the end of the property and nailed paper targets to some of the trees and began firing.

The weapons tore the bark off trees and seemed suitable for the IRA. After thirty minutes of practice, the soldiers liked the weapon.

The men were returning to their car when a crowd of novices gathered around them. Bart spoke up. "Mr. Collins, we're all praying for your success. God bless."

Collins walked over and put his arm on Bart's shoulder. "Thanks, Brother, we can use the prayers."

The next week Bart read this account in *The Irish Times*: 16/6/1921:

"US seized a consignment of Thompson sub-machine guns paid for by Americans. Captain Cronin and Major Dineen conducted Thompson training sessions. Collins trained with one in the Christian Brothers, from Marino in Dublin 3."

DEATH OF MICHAEL COLLINS

THE BRITISH ARRESTED MICHAEL Collins after the Easter Rising and sent him to Frongoch internment camp in Wales.

After the English released him, Collins became head of the Free State Army opposed to DeValera and the IRA. "Sure 'twas one of our own that shot him in his own county, the man who saved Ireland," "Who did it?" asked Dan Waddick, his friend. We'll probably never know," Jerry replied. "He was riding in an open Crossley Tender in a little place called Beal na Blath when some IRA men on a nearby hill shot at him and his men. His soldiers told him to get down on the ground but he stood up to fire back when a ricochet bullet hit him in the head, the only death in the shooting."

"Who fired the shot?" asked Waddick.

"The shooters took a vow of silence never to reveal the gunman's name," the IRA men answered.

After the assassination of Michael Collins in 1922, Ireland spiraled into a period of national mourning, unleashing a civil war between the Irish Free State, the party of Collins and Fianna Fail, (Soldiers of Destiny) the anti-treaty party of De Valera. Having met Collins during his practice with the Thompson submachine gun at Baldoyle, Bart was crestfallen by the murder of his hero.

Because the novitiate was a time of withdrawal from the world, the brothers had to receive permission from the novice master to attend Collins's funeral. Himself saddened by the death, Brother Chapman granted permission for any novice to attend the funeral and burial.

"Brothers," he said, "this is a sad day for our country—our leader's life has ended. Let us all pray for the soul of Michael Collins and for our suffering Ireland."

Mourners jammed the streets for the procession, among them many priests and brothers and nuns, all told some 500,000 mourners. Bart couldn't understand how a kind and loving Jesus could allow the death of the man who saved Ireland. To make matters worse, the only other politician of any consequence in the county was Eamon De Valera, a bitter enemy of Collins. Also, the murderous civil war was sure to drag on with no one of great stature to oppose De Valera.

After the assassination of Michael Collins in 1922, Ireland spiraled into a period of national mourning, unleashing a civil war between the Irish Free State, the party of Collins and Fianna Fail, (Soldiers of Destiny) the anti-treaty party of De Valera. Having met Collins during his practice with the Thompson submachine gun at Baldoyle, Bart was crestfallen by the murder of his hero.

Because the novitiate was a time of withdrawal from the world, the brothers had to receive permission from the novice master to attend Collins's funeral. Himself saddened by the death, Brother Chapman allowed any novice to attend the funeral and burial.

"Brothers," he said, "this is a sad day for our country—our leader's life has ended. Let us all pray, go into the chapel, and say a rosary for the soul of Michael Collins and for our suffering Ireland."

IN DINGLE

ON THE WAY TO Dingle, Browne snapped to his men. "Soon we'll destroy these ogham stones and monuments so revered by the Irish—once we finish off these rebels, ninety of them scattered throughout the countryside, and we'll smash every one of them down."

Private Dolan objected. "But these are relics from eons ago."

"No matter. All these Irish are pagans anyway," Browne said, "living in stone huts which gives them a place to hide guns."

From Tralee, Browne went to Galway where a local Catholic priest, Father Michael Griffin, was inciting his flock against England. To investigate the priest personally, Browne wore farmer's clothes to attend Father Griffin's Mass. Browne wore a heavy woolen shirt over gabardine trousers. But nothing could disguise his disfigurement, a patch of tight shiny skin where his right ear should be. He had lost his ear in the Great War at the Battle of the Somme when a German grenade seared his face, and only a surgeon's skill saved his life.

Father Griffin was a rebel priest, tending an I.R.A. man wounded seven times at the docks. Later he said a funeral Mass for Michael Walsh murdered by the British at the Old Malt House.

FATHER GRIFFIN

FATHER GRIFFIN FROM GALWAY was a rebel priest. He had tended an IRA man wounded seven times at the docks. Later he said a funeral Mass for Michael Walsh murdered by the British at the Old Malt House.

As a stranger in the church, Browne knew he would attract attention, so he tried to mimic the actions of those around him. He could make no sense of the priest's Latin mutterings, though the women in the congregation seemed to understand them and uttered responses. The priest spoke with his back to the people until it came time for the sermon when he turned to face them.

Tall and slender, Griffin projected a strong voice. "For over four hundred years since the time of Queen Elizabeth, Cromwell, and the Great Famine, we have been a subject people ruled by foreigners from across the sea. England had its own interests at heart, not ours. We have been England's breadbasket while our own people starved."

Despite himself, Browne found he was hanging on every word. The priest continued, "It is long past due that we rise up and shake off the tyrant's yoke. Only then will we be free to work in the Lord's vineyard as He wishes." The emotion stirred by Griffin's words simmered in the people around him. This was a dangerous man.

Browne made getting rid of the priest his next mission. To confront the priest directly was folly. He would only create another martyr in a country overflowing with them. He had to dispose of Griffin stealthily with no witnesses. To aid his cause, he had his men find out who in the parish was dying, in need of a visit from the priest. Their informants mentioned a

Widow Casey who lived by herself on the outskirts of the village. Perfect, Browne thought.

Two nights later just after dark, Browne gave a shilling to a boy who spoke Irish, his task

Father Michael Griffin Memorial

Photo courtesy of Graham Horn
http://www.geograph.ie/photo/1288863

Major Reginald Browne had been in command at the siege of Tralee where he had his men fire on churchgoers as they left Mass on All Saints Day, followed by a weeklong blockade of the city. A French journalist on the spot wrote, 'Volley after volley resounded to the terror of the people'. 'I do not remember, even in the [First World] War, having seen people as profoundly terrified as those of this small town, Tralee.' Only when the reporter wrote about the story to the embarrassment of England to the world did the Black and Tans relent. Browne also destroyed the local creamery depriving the people of butter and milk and costing many jobs.

Two nights later just after dark, Browne gave a shilling to a boy who spoke Irish, his task to fetch Father Griffin for a visit to Widow Casey in need of the Last Rites for the dying, a summons the priest wouldn't ignore.

Browne and two of his men waited near Widow Casey's in a ditch filled with bog water. Soon Father Griffin walked down the road carrying a suitcase with the sacred oils for anointing the dying. Jumping from the ditch, the soldiers tied the arms of the priest with rope, and Browne pressed a cloth dipped in chloroform to the priest's mouth rendering him unconscious.

"Go fetch the car from up the road," Browne ordered one of his soldiers. The night was starry with no moon, not another soul in sight. When the car arrived, the three soldiers lifted the priest into the boot.

"Drive to Barna. It's got a bog there that will be ideal," Browne said.

When they reached Barna, swamp water lay at their feet. They yanked the priest from the car.

"What are we going to do now?" asked William Dolan, RIC private.

"Shoot him. He's nothing but a rabble rouser," Browne replied.

"To kill a priest is a serious matter," Dolan said. He's just Catholic clergy who have fought us for years.

"Just follow orders and do your duty."

Father Griffin was beginning to come to around. "You'll never defeat us. You're only murderers in uniform."

Browne made Dolan fire the first shot hitting the priest full in the chest, Browne administering the final blow to the head. The three soldiers then rolled the body into the bog where it would lie hidden for days. On top of the priest, Browne pitched in the valise with the holy oils. "He has little use for it now."

Shooting

Led by Major Browne, three cars snaked up from British headquarters up the muddy road to Ballyristeen, a few miles from Dingle and just below Mount Brandon.

Ping. Ping. Clank. Clank. Ping. Ping. Clank. Clank. Whiz. A volley of shots rained down on the armored Black and Tan convoy, ricocheting among and scattering the soldiers. Private Dolan received a shot in his arm.

The road from Dingle to Ballyristeen runs north and east to the Aherne house ending in a steep hill like a green pyramid with sheep and cows clinging to it. Browne, short and stocky, wore a wound he would have forever. At the Somme in the Great War, the Germans seared his left ear with a mortar shell, leaving him with a patch of shiny red skin down one side of his face. Browne used his rifle butt to smash in the door of the Murphy house and hauled fourteen-year-old Bart from his family, his mother and father screaming as they chased the car up the road. "He's only fourteen."

Jerry was the only rebel in Dingle who was involved in the Rising. Long a friend of Thomas Ashe from the neighboring village of Lispole, the death of his friend spurred him on. Ashe had introduced him to Patrick Pearse, one of the leaders of the rebellion. Jerry had taken part in the Rising, badly wanting to be part of the "blood sacrifice" Pearse believed in. But Pearse convinced him to return to Dingle and work for the cause there where he had many rebel friends.

Two hundred miles from Dublin, Dingle learned of the Easter Rebellion only in bits and pieces, Jerry Murphy bearer of much of the news. Because the English in Kilmainham jail executed the rebels in secret, news of the shootings only trickled out, mainly through the comments of relatives of the martyrs because the authorities didn't want the populace stirred up against them.

Jerry Murphy was not surprised at the slaughter of the rebels. Because England wanted to join her in the Great War, the Irish hoped their desire might incline them to leniency, but this was not to be the case. U.S. President Woodrow Wilson didn't have his nation enter the war under General John Pershing until 1918, two years after the rebellion.

Jerry Murphy explained to his men that a Royal Commission seeking the reasons for the Rising concluded that the Dublin administration was lax in enforcing the law against the Irish. "Well," he said, "they certainly made up for that."

On a Friday, the Tans left their barracks and snaked up the mountain on the road to Ballyristeen.

In town Seamus Murdoch lit a peat fire behind his house, adding wood to make it smokier and alert the rebels to the movement of the enemy. Passing the Garfinny Bridge and the Garfinny Cemetery, Browne's lorry arrived at the Aherne house to question them: "Have you seen the rebels up here?"

"No," Paudie Aherne answered, his wife Breeda standing behind them. "We've seen neither hide nor hair of them."

"Mind you tell the truth," Browne warned, "or it will go hard for you and yours."

When the soldiers left, Breeda said to her husband, "We must be careful or they'll come back to haunt us."

"Yes, Breeda, but we can't inform on our neighbors."

High on a hill overlooking the road, Dan Waddick yelled to his companions, "The Tans are coming up the road."

Then Browne used his rifle butt to smash in the door of the Murphy house and hauled fourteen-year-old Bart from his family, his mother and father screaming as they chased the car up the road. They shoved the boy into the lead lorry and then drove half a mile more to the end of the road when the soldiers jumped from their cars. A bullet pinged from the hills above past them.

It was a raw, cold day. Speaking into a megaphone, Browne roared,

"Hold your fire, Jerry Murphy, unless you want to see your brother a corpse."

At the top of the road in the last cottage, Breeda Aherne held her husband back from helping Jerry: "Paddy, if they shoot you who will raise our children. Sure, they'll only murder you too."

"You're right, Breeda. But it hurts to see a neighbor slaughtered."

Silence then rained down from above where a few sheep looked at the intruders curiously.

"Maybe your brother doesn't care if you die," Browne smirked to Bart.

Then a lone form rose against the gray sky and made its way toward them. Bart screamed up, "Jerry don't come. They'll shoot me anyway."

Browne smashed him with a rifle butt sending him sprawling into the mud. "Shut up, you tinker."

But the figure still came on. Bart was crying now, choking on his sobs.

When Jerry came within shooting distance, one soldier raised his rifle, but Browne barked, "No. I'll administer the coup de grace myself. I'll enjoy it. I should have gotten him at the GPO. I missed him the first time but not this time."

Jerry stumbled forward, his blue eyes hollow and defeated, after two years of running from these bastards. Browne grabbed Mick and shoved him back down the road to home. "You priest killer," Jerry yelled at Browne.

To two soldiers Browne said, "Make him kneel in memory of his precious Father Griffin."

Jerry resisted. Still standing, he screamed at Browne, "Do it now, you bastard."

"As you say," Browne replied.

Bart froze in terror as he watched Brown raise his blue-black Webley revolver and shot Jerry in the forehead, smashing him backward.

Just then a spray of bullets from up on the mountain scattered the soldiers, Browne shouting to his men, "Leave the body here, a lesson to the rest."

Ignoring the bullets, Bart ran back to his brother "Oh, Jerry, God help us," but he could do nothing for him. Jerry was gone.

In town Bridie Kevane heard the news of Jerry's death, but she wanted to see for herself. When she met Bart stumbling and crying on the road, she knew the story was true. "I loved him. Where is he now?" She went to the body and kissed her dead man lying on the road, blood leaking from his head. "I had hoped you would be my husband."

Bart said, "Clear out, Bridie. They may shoot you too. They killed women and children in the Rising in Dublin."

REACTION IN DINGLE

The people in Dingle studied all the comings and goings of the Black and Tans from their brick barracks in the heart of town. No soldiers would go out after dark with the curfew.

The exception was Major Browne who walked his bulldog Winston every evening. By this time, news of Father Griffin's death had reached the town still reeling from the shooting of Jerry Murphy.

The Gun

THE NEXT NIGHT, TELLING no one, young Bart took a circuitous path to the school of the Christian Brothers in Dingle to seek help. Rumor spread that the brothers had guns squirreled away. Bart knocked on the wooden door, and Brother Hennessy, his maths teacher, answered it. Hennessy brought Bart into a small room dominated by a crucifix. "As I said at your brother's wake, I'm sorry about your loss, but you shouldn't be out at curfew. These Tans would just as soon shoot you as look at you."

"I know, Brother, but there's something I have to do."

"What?"

"I need a gun."

Hennessy turned pale. "Bart, sure you're too young to be a soldier. Your family couldn't bear the loss of another son. Jesus, Mary, and Joseph. Hasn't there been enough suffering in your house?"

"Brother, I need a gun."

Exasperated with the young man, Hennessy said, "I'll speak to the community here in the house and get their views. Come back a week from tonight and I'll have an answer for you."

"Thanks, Brother."

WAITING

During the next few days, Hennessy floated the young man's request to the seven other brothers. Though all felt sad for the Murphy family, some brothers opposed giving young Bart the weapon, fearful of English retaliation.

The community decided to hold a meeting about Bart's request for a gun. Their opinions varied, some fearing that the Tans would burn down their school if they learned that the young man had received the gun from them. Brother Perry said, "Blood will have blood."

Brother Fearon replied "the words of Shakespeare a bloody Englishman. Aren't they the very ones persecuting us? Bart Murphy is one of our own. Let's give him the rifle."

The superior, Brother Carr, spoke up. "I'm against giving a lad of fourteen a rifle. But majority rules. After praying each of us will write 'yes' or 'no' for giving Bart the gun and place our response on a piece of paper on the altar."

The vote fell five to two for passing on the rifle. "Let's say a rosary now—that we've made the right choice," said Brother Carr. "And not a word to anyone, not even our closest friends."

Effectively dodging the barracks on Main Street, the following week Bart made his way back to the monastery of the Christian Brothers. Brother Hennessy was waiting for Bart with a candle to see in the darkened barn. He handed the boy a Smith and Enfield rifle wrapped in oilcloth.

Brother Hennessy also gave him a box with eight rounds of

ammunition. "Be careful, Bart, or else you'll land the Tans down on us. If you're captured, tell the Tans a farmer found the gun and wanted to turn it into the barracks for fear the soldiers might discover it."

"Yes, brother, I'll be very careful, taking a roundabout way home. With the curfew on and people afraid of being shot, the streets are deserted."

"That may be, Bart, but the Tans have snipers who would just as soon shoot you as look at you. Your family can't bear the loss of another son."

"Yes, Brother, our house still smells of roses, snuff, and wax from the candles around Jerry's body."

PRACTICE SHOOTING

BART HAD FOUND A small lake, called a corrie, formed by seepage behind a hill on Mount Brandon which would minimize any sound. He carried the rifle in an old potato sack that he found hidden in a pile of peat turf from behind the family cottage. To help him learn how to use the Lee Enfield gun, Bart recruited an old soldier, Jim Comack, who had fought in the failed Fenian Rebellion in 1867. Comack showed him how to load the ten bullets and then instructed him to shoot at tin cans the old man he had brought from home. Bart's first attempt landed only a few feet in front of him "Jesus, lad, you almost took your toe off. Stand with your feet spread apart for balance."

Bart's next shots were closer even nicking one of the cans.

"Better, lad, but still not good enough. Let me show you." Comack hit the cans on his first try, scattering them among the rocks.

Imitating the old man, Bart got better. "An improvement, we'll come back tomorrow. How many bullets do you have?"

"A boxful."

"That will be plenty."

The next evening Bart and Comack repeated their practice until the old man was happy.

From his sack Bart pulled out a jug of poitin. "This is for you, Mr. Comack, moonshine made by a farmer up the road."

"Thanks, lad. You're a man after my own heart. You realize I haven't asked you what the rifle is for. I don't want to know. Keep this between ourselves. Tell no one else, mind. We have informers even among our own people."

Browne's Movements

Bart's next step was to learn more about the habits of Major Browne.

Seamus Murdoch, two years older than Bart, lived in a cottage directly across the road from the Tan barracks. Bart approached Seamus, "I have a big favor to ask you, and won't feel bad if you turn me down."

"What is it then so?" asked Seamus.

"I'm going to shoot Browne. I've practiced using a Lee Enfield with the help of Jim Comack, and I'm ready."

"Jesus, Bart. You have reason enough, but they would suspect you first thing after they murdered Jerry. Where did you get the gun?"

"I don't want to say to protect my friends. There is much danger in this, Seamus, as you can imagine. So give it a good think."

"I will. Every evening just after curfew begins Browne takes his bulldog Winston for a walk down to the harbor and back. Because the Tans have boarded up the windows of the barracks, it's hard for them to see out. This could be done. I've been too fearful to do it."

"Seamus, not to worry about being scared. I'm frightened too, but I'm going to do this. My only worry is me ma and da."

"The Tans shot my uncle in Tralee, but I'm afraid. These bastards are terrible vengeful. Me Ma and Da are gone, so I'm worried only about myself."

"Take a day to consider it and we'll talk again. We'll meet in the field beyond your house next evening."

The next evening Bart and his friend walked the long way around to the field beyond Seamus's cottage where peat was stored like logs. "Well, I've thought it over and I'm in, God help me."

"Good, we'll follow Browne for a few nights and get his route down pat. Every night at the beginning of curfew, he walks his bloody bulldog to the harbor and back. With the curfew, there will be nobody else about."

Browne's History

Just as the Great War was engulfing Europe, Reginald Browne, son of a widower, served in the British infantry. His younger brother Percival worked in the steel mills. Following closely his brother's letters from the Front, he and his mother felt anxious when the writing stopped. Afraid that Reginald had been killed in battle, the two of them scoured casualty lists in the *Daily Mail*. Finally, a letter from a nurse at the Front reported that Reginald was alive, but that a German mortar had severed his right ear and burned his face. His brother, young Percival volunteered for the infantry.

While Reginald recuperated at home, he spewed venom against the Irish and Germans. "Goddamn Irish and Germans, I hate them. The captain sent me out to rescue three Irishmen who made it back to the line without a scratch. When you're in battle, Percival, avoid the feckin Irish. They aren't even good soldiers." Following his brother's advice, Percival returned from the war safely minus his right ear burned off by a grenade.

Reginald Browne received a commendation for bravery and a promotion to Major. At home he grew restless, and when the Anglo-Irish War erupted, he and Percival became members of the Black and Tans with their uniforms of black and khaki. Seething with a desire for revenge, he became commander at Tralee. Percival joined the army in Dublin, a rebel stronghold.

CONSCIENCE

BART SUFFERED PANGS OF conscience for what he was about to do. Even though Browne was a bad man, he still was a man for whose death Bart would be responsible, breaking the Sixth Commandment, "Thou shalt not kill." But all he had to do was to think of Jerry's death on the road and the murder of Father Griffin to soothe his scruples.

REVENGE

BROWNE WAS SUSPICIOUS. THERE had been no retaliation for the murder of Father Griffin or Jerry Murphy. As he prepared for his nightly walk with his dog in tow, he checked to see if there were any candles lit in the cottages along his route. Darkness covered everything. The only sounds were the banging of small boats together, seagulls squawking, and sails blowing the wind.

Browne walked with a rifle under one arm and a lantern in the other down the path leading to the harbor. Winston trailed behind his master. Suddenly a gray wharf rat shot out behind some wooden pilings triggering an explosion from the dog. "Winston, you bastard, get back here." The bulldog crushed the skull of the rat in one bite, distracting Browne for a minute or two. Bart threw a sack of mutton at the dog drawing him away from his master.

Bart told Seamus, "Let's go," and they jumped from their hiding place.

Browne had his back to the water when he saw the two men. "Who goes there? I'll shoot you for breaking curfew."

Bart had resolved to shoot his enemy face to face. "You murdered my brother."

Before Browne could raise his rifle, Bart shot him full in the chest, pitching him backward on the dock. When Seamus was about to fire, Bart yelled, "No, I want this to be entirely on me." Bart walked to the corpse to make sure Browne was dead. He was.

Seamus, long a boats-man, often went out with the fleet to catch cod and the odd salmon, so he knew the bay. He showed Bart how to make slipknots. The two of them tied long flat stones around each of Browns' arms and legs, so that he would sink easier. They dumped the corpse into a rowboat along with his lamp and shoved the body over the side into more twenty meters of water. Bart then threw his rifle and bullets as far as he could into the dark water of Dingle Bay. The dog they let go.

"Seamus, we've done what we came for. Take the long way around to get home and not a word to anyone, mind. Because of the curfew no one has seen us. Thanks for all your help. We've gotten rid of a killer, God rest his murdering soul."

When Bart arrived home, his mother said. "Where have you been? Sure, you put the heart cross ways in us with the curfew and all, and we just after burying Jerry."

"I finished the barn for Brother Hennessy. He was happy with the work."

Bart was glad he had gotten revenge for Jerry. But another side of him felt guilty. He would attend confession on Saturday and repent his sin.

CONFESSION

EVERY SATURDAY CATHOLICS IN Dingle would attend Confession at St. Mary's Church to prepare themselves for Mass and Holy Communion the next day. After blessing himself with holy water, Bart left the alms in the poor box under the stained glass windows, and hesitant to reveal his sin, Bart trembled in the line for confession. Bart knew that the pastor, Canon McMahon, held it against Catholics that in 1845 Prime Minister Robert Peel donated 27 Million pounds to Ireland to establish Maynooth Seminary. Never the kindest priest in the best of times, the canon bore little resemblance to the forgiving Jesus of the New Testament— as if he regarded every sin as a personal affront.

Nervous at the reception he might receive, Bart stood at the back of the line behind a dozen old biddies driving him crazy by knocking their rosaries against the wooden pews. Bart hoped that Canon McMahon would be in a good mood. But such was not to be the case.

Bart knelt down for confession and recited the formula he had learned in grammar school. Because Dingle is a Gaeltacht (Irish speaking) area, Bart spoke in Irish.

> A Dhia, tá doilíos croí orm
> gur chuir mé fearg ort,
> agus tá fuath fíreannach agam
> do mo pheacaí thar gach olc eile,
> a Dhia, a thuilleas mo ghrá go hiomlán
> mar gheall ar do mhaitheas gan teorainn;
> agus tá rún daingean agam,
> le cúnamh do naomhghrásta

gan fearg a chur ort arís go brách,
agus mo bheatha a leasú.
Amen.

Translation: "Bless me, Father, for I have sinned. It has been 3 weeks since my last confession. I shot Major Browne. These are my sins. For these and all my past sins, I am very sorry."

When Bart said "I shot Major Browne," it was as if he had set off a bomb in the confessional. Jumping from his side of the wooden box, Canon McMahon screamed "You did what? You idjit bringing the Tans down on us."

Bart had had enough, bolting from the church onto Main Street. He had learned from his religion classes that the priest had broken the seal of confession, never to reveal a penitent's sins.

"Get back here, you," the priest yelled. Bart kept on running.

Trip to Dublin

Having accepted his application to the Order, the brothers sent Bart on his way to Dublin. Even though they had given him the rifle, the brothers in community never knew he had used it to shoot Major Browne. The brothers in Dingle approved Bart's application unanimously. Their seminary, Baldoyle, was two hundred miles away where Bart would receive his religious training and teaching qualifications. With the Black and Tans probing the area, Bart and his father knew to be careful.

TINKERS

JUST AS THEY PASSED the ambush site at Kilmichael, Bart and his father met a caravan of tinkers coming towards them, six people riding in a cart pulled by two black and white ponies. "Da, get off the road so these tinkers can go through."

"Right you are, Bart. They're a tough looking crowd. They're speaking in *cant* or *shelta,* their own language. You can 't trust them; sure, they'd steal the eye out of your head."

"Not many of them around us at home, probably because we're so far from big towns."

Smoking a clay pipe, a man of middle age was driving the cart, his wife and children riding in back. "Do ye have any money that I can use to buy food for the little ones?"

"No we don't," Bart's father said.

"We're on our way to a stone shifting in Skibbereen," the tinker said. "We move the large stones to the river so the people will have good weather. By the way, I've a pretty lass here that would give either of you—or both—a tumble for a few shillings. "Sheila, come here. Let these two gentlemen have a look at you." A girl with raven hair in braids came from the back of the wagon and sat near her father. Wearing a green dress, she was pretty but unwashed.

Blushing, Bart stammered "No."

Seeing the young man's discomfort, the tinker father said, "If it's your first time, she'll help you. She's easy with men."

"No," Bart's father said. "We must be going."

As they rode away, Bart said, "Isn't it terrible altogether that a man would sell his child like that?" But Bart and his father both knew this was a common tinker practice.

"We don't know how the tinkers started up, whether or not Cromwell drove them from large estates. They look like us with their light-colored hair and fair skin. We'll say a prayer for them and make our way to Dublin."

Mission – Teaching Post

Having completed his training at Baldoyle, Bart was ready for his first teaching post. He had had 3 years of teaching practice. He hoped it would be in Ireland. But instead headquarters assigned him to Boys' Central High School in Butte, Montana, home to many Irish immigrants who worked in the copper mines there. The head of the order in Dublin wanted anyone involved with the IRA out of the country far from English control.

Never possessing a strong constitution, Bart suffered lung problems from the harsh Montana winters. His health became so bad the American provincial, Br. Delaney, traveled to Butte to speak with him. "Bart, you've been in hospital twice in three months, so we've decided to transfer you to Rice High School in New York where the climate is more moderate."

"Brother," said Bart, "I know you mean well, but I'm happy here and don't wish to go to New York or anywhere else."

"Bart, you're under a vow of obedience. We need you in our schools and your health is important to us and to you to train our boys."

BART MURPHY IN NEW YORK

BUT YEARS LATER IN the infirmary of the Irish Christian Brothers in West Park, New York, eighty miles from New York City, Brother Bart Murphy was very sick with emphysema, perhaps a result of his time living in Ireland's damp climate and in Montana's cold. In his early eighties and after sixty-two years in the congregation, much of it spent as a teacher and librarian at Rice High School in Harlem, he was tired of that burden from his youth that haunted all his nights and days, yearning for the release that only death can bring. Rumor had persisted about Bart's involvement in the IRA.

RELIGIOUS LIFE

Bart was scrupulous in his religious duties rising at 5:40 a.m. for morning prayers, meditation, and Mass. Only once a month on Saturday afternoons would he deviate from the community schedule. That day he would sneak out of the school and catch the subway downtown to attend a meeting of Clann na Gael (The Irish Family), a group of Irish fanatics determined to destroy England. Even to his Old-Country friends and fellow religious, he never told of his membership. The group was happy to have a religious with them and wanted to elect him president, but he knew Americans might view the group as subversive and leave him open to FBI deportation.

The Superior, Brother Wight, was a brothers' brother, principal of Rice High School. One of his problems in dealing with the Irish brothers was that many of them were sent to America to get them away from the

English authorities during the Anglo-Irish war, and they harbored bitter memories of the Old Country.

The Irish are good at fighting among themselves especially in regards to their attitudes toward England.

The first Irish brothers came to America in 1920, a novice master and his assistant both died in the spring of 1920 in Kingston, New York. The bodies were reinterred in West Park. The cemetery was for the brothers only.

Before he took his siesta, Bart glanced across the sprawling Hudson, 7/8th of a mile to the Vanderbilt Mansion, gleaming white and surrounded by manicured lawns and gardens with a profusion of flowers. Vanderbilt and his wife had hired an agent who ransacked Europe for ornate German and Italian furniture and tapestries. Upon his death, Vanderbilt's wife put the estate up for sale. During World War II the Secret Service lived there.

Father Divine, a controversial Black minister from Harlem, wrote to FDR to see if he would mind having him for a neighbor. Because he was racist, Roosevelt minded very much, and he convinced Mrs. Vanderbilt to make the estate a New York historical site, taking the property off the market—which she did. Because he was a bigamist, the authorities allowed his out of New York only on Sundays.

Percival Browne's Revenge

Major Browne had a younger brother Percival who had also joined the Black and Tans. Stationed in Dublin when he learned of his brother's disappearance, he petitioned headquarters to transfer to Dingle. He had murder in his heart. When he arrived in Dingle, young Browne questioned two farmers in town, shooting and killing both because they gave him no information. Once the violence began, many townspeople fled on boats or sought refuge in the mountains.

Two later events stirred up the rebels in Dingle. Terence MacSwiney, the Lord Mayor of Cork, died in prison on a hunger strike protesting wrongful imprisonment. Also, Kevin Barry, an eighteen-year-old Dublin boy, received a sentence of hanging for his role in the deaths of three British soldiers. In Dingle Percival Browne did find an informer, Tom Clancy, who said, "My money is on Jerry Murphy whom the major executed a few days after his disappearance."

"Clancy," Browne said, "be sure you're telling me the truth. If not, I'll be sure to finish you off just like those two I killed." Browne paid Clancy five pounds for his information.

Then finally a miracle. England pulled all the Black and Tans home from Ireland because the world press reviled them, robbing Browne of his chance to avenge his brother.

After leaving the army, Browne worked in the steel mills in Birmingham, England with his desire for revenge still consuming him.

After five months Browne wrote to Clancy in Dingle sending him ten pounds. He learned that Bart Murphy had joined the Christian Brothers and moved to New York. Browne thought "That bastard, a murderer, hiding under the cloak of religion."

DISSENSION

SOME SEMI-RETIRED AND ILL brothers lived in the novitiate with fifteen young candidates in a large frame house St. Mary's in West Park, New York, in the Hudson Valley. At breakfast one day an elderly Canadian, Brother Verde, asked, "Why do you Irish blame England for the Famine and for the Rising?"

"From 1846 until 1851, they burned our homes and stole our crops and livestock while our own people starved. They shipped our food to England under armed guard," replied Bart Murphy. "They murdered my brother."

The Irish brought typhus and death to Grosse Ile," Br. Verde charged.

"The Brits destroyed our land and evicted us—almost two million Irish—seized our food for themselves while our country starved. It might have been worse except for the good Quakers who established soup kitchens, redeemed fishermen's nets and clothes from pawn, and taught our women and children," Bart said.

Br. Verde said, "Bart you brought disease and death to Canada. Those who didn't die in Ireland passed away in coffin ships"

"You're blaming the victims. Marita Foster, a historian explains that the number of dead from the coffin ships would form a continuous line from Ireland to Grosse Ile. If it weren't for Dr. Douglas, the Grey Nuns, and local priests, the disaster would have been worse," Bart said.

Usually quiet, Brother Angelus spoke up. "At our school in Skibbereen, the brothers served meals every day to starving children. During the Rising we hid guns for the rebels under the altar cloths."

Bart said "The English looked upon the Famine as a dispensation of Providence, punishment for our Catholicism."

Brother Wight, the superior, said "We must stop this discussion. It leads only to argument and bad feeling."

With their motto, "If you have to say something, say nothing" the Irish excel in secrecy, keeping mum with the English and their informers spying around them. Bart had kept his own counsel from the time he was a sixteen-year-old novice at the brothers' seminary in Baldoyle. Both Old Country and Yank brothers thought him a kindly old religious. But if the tortured minister Dimmesdale in the *Scarlet Letter* bore the letter "A" hidden on his chest, Bart wore the letter "M" for murderer under his black habit.

As Bart dozed off, he had his terrible dream about Jerry's death. As a fourteen-year-old- boy, he idolized his older brother Jerry, but their parents lived in constant fear for their son's life.

Brother Thomas Pierce bounced into Bart's room just in time to end his nightmare. "Bart, do you want me to pray with you?"

"No, Tom," Bart yelled, "I've already said my beads today," holding up his black congregation beads as proof.

No brother was as irritating to Bart as Tom, always chipper, darting around like a squirrel. One of his quirks was peeling an orange in one fluid movement cutting out one long piece of the skin providing the novices with entertainment. Tom turned up the volume of his hearing aid, Bart chuckling to himself because he always spoke softly to his nemesis just to provoke him into raising the volume of his hearing aid and then yelling. Tom taught catechism in nearby Kingston and was proud of himself for still working while these other old men—like Bart—were clinging to life in their hospital beds. Rubbing it in, Tom said, "Don't you wish you were still working in the Lord's vineyard?"

As Tom closed the door, Bart heaved a blue vase full of water and daisies, spreading the mess on the floor.

An hour later the Brother Superior, William Wight, who had been Bart's superior, a thick-set New Yorker in his fifties, came to visit Bart, part of making his afternoon rounds of the old brothers. "What happened here?" Wight asked.

"I'm sorry, William. Sure, I got so mad at Tom that I threw the vase and flowers at the door after he left."

"Not to worry," Wight said, chuckling. "There's plenty of life in you yet. Tom would try even the Lord's patience. One of the novices will clean it up."

SCARE

ONE MORNING AT BREAKFAST a black car arrived at St Mary's. The brothers, thirty of them, were having breakfast in a long dining hall. From the car two men with crew cuts and suits, mirror images of each other, stepped out. One man knocked on the door which a novice answered. "We're here to see the priest in charge," the first man said. Lay people didn't understand that brothers were not priests and did not administer the sacraments.

"Please come in" the novice answered. "I'll get him for you." Brother Wight arose from the table to meet the men.

"Father, I'm Secret Service agent Mason, and this is agent Thorn. We're stationed at the President Roosevelt's compound, Springwood, across the Hudson. We're here to investigate a car that comes here from 9W, and we worry about the President's safety."

Bart Murphy heard the conversation. Breaking into a cold sweat, Bart worried about the pro-Irish group *Clann na Gael* (our Irish family) of which he had been a member in New York. Brother Wight thought for a minute. "That must be Father Barry who comes from the Redemptorist seminary at Esopus to say Mass for us. He is here right now and can confirm this. Do you wish to speak with him? And please have a cup of coffee with us."

Over coffee, the two agents talked with Father Barry who satisfied them. "Thanks, Father, any threat to the President is a concern to us."

When the agents left, Bart Murphy breathed a sigh of relief.

EMBARRASSMENT OF A NOVICE

AT A COMMUNITY BREAKFAST of all the brothers during which a novice would read aloud from a spiritual book, like the Lives of the Saints, Brother Verde asked all the senior brothers to leave the dining hall so he could lacerate a Chicagoan Brother Denis for his weak oral reading. "Your reading is like a fly buzzing against a window screen. No one can make a bit of sense about what you're saying." Adding to Denis's misery was the mean reaction of some of the other novices, happy that it was him and not themselves whom Verde pilloried.

The castigation mortified the novice, a first-year college student to be subjected to these insults. At Leo High School in Chicago, he was a four-year honor student and a state scholarship winner. Verde told him to do the reading again. In his mind he said, "Fuck you, Brother." Just then another novice spoke up, a fellow Chicagoan, Dominic, seemingly shy with pimples splotching his face. "Brother, you're not helping Denis, simply embarrassing him in front of all of us. Why don't you take him aside and give him some instruction? Would Jesus teach this way?"

Dominic had turned the tables. Here was Brother Verde, a senior brother, being reprimanded by a novice. "God bless him," Denis thought. "Hope he doesn't get in trouble."

Denis grew angrier the longer he thought about his humiliation. He would leave West Park, and go to DePaul or Loyola, where many of his friends were already enrolled. He knocked on Brother Wight's door and said "I want to leave. I'll call home to my parents and let them know I'm coming."

"You can't leave. You're under first vows."

"Watch me."

"Denis, you're a model novice and a fine student."

"I want to leave."

"What brought this on?"

The novice explained the story, that he had been mortified for his weak reading.

Wight was angry with Brother Verde. He thought here we are hoping these novices will stay and Verde will drive them out. "Denis, I'll speak with Brother Verde. This won't happen again. In the meantime, see Brother Angelus for help with your reading."

Wild Dogs

One afternoon Bart was sunning himself on the front porch, when two wild dogs were pursuing a terrified fawn across the lawn. Bart ran into the house for help from Brother Dan Crimmins, a woodsman, and a crack shot. "Dan, two dogs are about to kill a deer." Crimmins hustled into the kitchen where a .22 was hanging behind a door. Usually, dogs travel as part of a larger pack. Storming outside, Crimmins saw the lead dog, a black mastiff, gaining on the fawn. Hiding behind a brown boulder and a wide oak tree, he shot the pursuer who limped away. He then shot the second dog, an outsized boxer while the fawn loped safely into the woods on the other side of the lawn.

Both dogs were only wounded which made them more dangerous. Crimmins followed their trail of blood on the far side of the cemetery. Thrashing his way through the woods, Dan heard snarling and fighting just ahead, a sign of a larger pack. The leader of the pack, the mastiff, was an apricot brindle and larger than the other dogs. He had yellow eyes and a slavering mouth, signs of disease from rabies. The mastiff came straight for Dan who didn't look the dog in the eye, a sign of aggression. Tripping on a hidden tree root, Crimmins stumbled and triggered a leap from the dog, but Dan rose in time to wound it with a bullet to the head. Limping badly, the boxer fled into the bush. The next day Dan found the boxer dead. He then buried both dogs.

Dan Crimmins came to Bart Murphy who had watched most of the scene: "Bart, but for you there would be one dead fawn. You saved that one."

The praise pleased Bart.

From then on the brothers watched for wild dogs. Brother Crimmins called Sheriff Olson in New Paltz and told him about the dogs.

"Damn city folks," Olson complained," they come up here on vacation with puppies and let them loose in the woods when they're full grown, creating havoc for the farmers. Many of these dogs contract rabies from fox bites. I'll have to warn your neighbors."

The other concerns were the chickens and turkeys that old Brother Camillus raised that would be easy prey for the dogs. On his next trip to town, Crimmins bought a .22 rifle for the old brother and taught him how to load and use it.

WIGHT AND BROTHER ANGELUS

As MUCH AS WIGHT loved Bart, he always suspected that something was gnawing at the man's soul. But Bart was so private that he dare not intrude on his suffering. Wight sensed that it had much to do with Ireland. Every seventh summer when Bart took his sabbatical leave to Ireland, he would be excited and eager. But when he returned from the Old Country, he would fall into a deep depression from which only the routines of school and prayer would revive him.

Brother Angelus had been a friend of Bart since their training at Baldoyle in Ireland, so Brother Wight came to him for help. "Angelus, Bart seems depressed. What can we do to help him?" Angelus put his work down to face William.

"I haven't told this to a soul, but it may help. When Bart was fourteen, two years before he joined the order, the Black and Tans shot and killed his brother Jerry right before his eyes. The Tans used Bart as hostage and the poor man has never forgiven himself. In his mind Jerry died for him. There's more, but Bart has never told me the rest. Sure, they were going to kill Jerry in any case because he was IRA. What you might do is find some kind Old Country priest to talk with him and settle his mind. The Redemptorists right down the road are good men, but are mostly German or Yank. Bart needs an Irishman, someone who understands "The Troubles.""

BACK TO SCHOOL

AT RICE HIGH SCHOOL in the middle of the black belt, Brother Murphy taught English and Latin five periods a day to the sons of Irish immigrants, "narrowbacks," a term of mild derision used by immigrants because unlike their parents their children had not worked on the docks, digging canals, or in construction, physically demanding jobs. Bart especially liked the freshmen because it took them longer to discover how easy his discipline was. Awed by a faculty of all males, unlike the sisters who had taught them in grammar school, they fell into line easily. Only rarely did he have to bring out his brown leather strap from his drawer and bang it off his desk to scare them. The strap was equipment necessary for discipline.

THE PRESIDENT

OVER THE YEARS THE novices had carved out a walking path from the novitiate over 9 W to the Hudson. Brother Dan had cut through the sumac trees and bushes and cleared a flat space for swimming and for the old brothers to sit and to enjoy the breeze wafting from the river. On a Sunday afternoon Bart and Brother Carthage were sitting there when Roosevelt's white yacht, the *Potomac*, came sailing by, the President with a light summer fedora and smoking a cigarette held at a jaunty angle.

Bart said, "If I had a gun, I'd take a shot at the devil."

"You'd shoot the President?" Carthage said.

"Yes, indeed," Bart said. "Think of all those narrowbacks who have died because of the Japs or Nazis. Thank God, De Valera wouldn't permit such a thing in Ireland. Sure 'twas Churchill who dragged Roosevelt into the war. And it was Churchill and Lloyd George who got Collins to sign the peace treaty—'I'm signing my death warrant' Collins said, and he was right, assassinated two years later."

This part of the Hudson was seminary row with religious houses of training up and down both sides of the river because religious orders paid no taxes. Besides the brothers, were the Redemptorists, the Blessed Sacrament Fathers, the Marist Fathers, the Jesuits, and the Mother Cabrini sisters. Roosevelt waved to the brothers. Trailing the yacht by a few hundred yards, was a Coast Guard cutter for security—although the President scoffed at the idea that he needed protection on the water. But speculation surfaced that the Germans or the Japanese planned to build a midget submarine for one or two men that would enter the mouth of the Atlantic and make its way north to the Roosevelt home in Hyde Park to kill him.

Two events encouraged Irish militant groups in America like Clann n Gael (Our Irish Family). In June 1942, a Nazi u boat (German <u>unterseeboot—</u>" under seas boat") had penetrated American waters and landed four spies at Amagansett off Long Island. These men had $175,000 in cash, and explosives and detonators. Spotted and interrogated by a Coast Guard lookout, the men fled to New York City.

The Nazis launched a second attempt at sabotage, one on June 12, 1942, when u-boat submarine U-202 dropped off 4 Germans. Coastguardsman John Cullen intercepted them and informed his superiors. After burying explosives and weapons on the beach, the men escaped and made their way to New York City. On June 16, 1942, another group of four spies landed off Ponte Vedra, Florida, just south of Jacksonville.

George Dasch, leader of the spies, got cold feet and confessed the plots to FBI Assistant Director E. M. Ladd in Washington. Afraid that a civilian court might be too lenient, Roosevelt had Congress create a military tribunal which met in the Department of Justice Building in Washington. The tribunal found six of the defendants guilty, executed them, and buried them in a potter's field in Anacostia, Washington. Because they had helped reveal the plot, the President commuted Dasch's sentence to thirty years and his assistant Burger to life.

When Hitler learned of the scheme, he was furious with Admiral Canaris, Nazi Director of Intelligence, and forbade any more attempts at subversion in America. In 1948 President Truman granted executive clemency to the two spies with the proviso that they return to the American zone in Germany.

Despite J. Edgar Hoover's attempt at a news blackout of the incident, word eventually leaked out.

FDR Grave

Photo courtesy of PresidentsUSA.net
http://www.presidentsusa.net/fdrgravesite.html

There was mystery about Roosevelt's death. In the company of his daughter, mistress, and doctor, Roosevelt suffered a cerebral hemorrhage and died. The brothers from West Park had observed the train bearing his body stop on the New York Central tracks and travel by a back road to the cemetery.

Springwood, the name for the Roosevelt compound, was hidden from West Park by a turn in the river. Having visited there often, Bart didn't need to see the place to visualize it—a quarter mile from the river surrounded by thousands of trees donated by Syracuse University. Two palm trees flanked the front portico where the President gave his presidential acceptance speeches.

As they drove to the Rose Garden, Bart thought of all the reasons for hating Roosevelt. He had pulled Joe Kennedy back from ambassador to England because he was pro-Nazi. Churchill hated the Irish and with Lloyd-George influenced Michael Collins to sign the treaty which cost him his life. Collins said, "I'm signing my death warrant."

Not far from the house is the Rose Garden where the President and Eleanor lie buried next to a gravestone of white Vermont marble. Eleanor wished for some quote like "We have nothing to fear except fear itself," but FDR left specific instructions in his will that only his and his wife's years of birth and death mark the stone.

Because he had never learned how to drive, Bart asked Brother Dan to take him. They drove south to Newburgh and crossed the river to Poughkeepsie and then north to Hyde Park. Brother Dan said," Why do you want to go there?"

"I have my reasons," Bart replied

Located ninety miles north of New York City, the Roosevelt estate is on Route 9 Boston Post Road about a half mile from the highway. Next to the presidential library lie the gravestones of Franklin and Eleanor. Brother Dan pulled into a parking lot next to the Rose Garden having received instructions from Bart. "If a Park Service man comes close, honk the horn twice as a warning."

Bart stepped over a low hedge and walked to the gravestone. Unzipping his pants, he urinated on the grave, splashing water on himself. He heard a car horn beep twice.

"Father, what are you doing in there?" asked a Park Services Security man.

"Saying a prayer for our dear dead President," Bart replied.

"Please get out of there," the man said. "No one is allowed beyond the hedge."

Bart replied, "Pog Ma Thoin. (Kiss my Ass)."

BROWNE IN BROOKLYN

ONCE BROWNE LEARNED FROM Tom Clancy that Bart Murphy had relocated to New York, he moved his operations there. With a good reference from a Birmingham steel mill, Browne got a job with the Flatbush Steel Mill in Brooklyn. He fit in easily though he hated his fellow workers, most of them Irish.

From them he learned that the Christian Brothers had schools in Harlem and the Bronx.

He tried Harlem first, Rice High School, and discovered that Murphy taught there. He made an appointment with the principal to survey the place. Taking the subway to 124th and Lennox Avenue, he found the school, a five-story building of red brick surrounded by brownstones where Negroes lived which made him wonder if there were problems between them and the Irish kids in the school, a question he would pose to the principal.

Browne knew that Clancy, now an old man, was in Dingle; he would have to find out where Bart Murphy was. West Park was out of the question at least for a while because he was known there. He called Rice High School and asked if Brother Murphy was available.

The secretary answered, "Yes, sir. He's here right now." Perfect. They were both in the same place.

Brother Wight, the principal, a burly man in his forties, welcomed Browne into his office filled with pictures of Jesus and Mary and of Irishman Edmund Rice, founder of the order. "How can I help you?" Wight asked.

"My names is Percival Browne, and I'd like to enroll my son here.

He's in eighth grade at Our Lady of Perpetual Help in Brooklyn, but I'm worried about the neighborhood having so many Negroes."

"No problems with our neighbors, many of whom are enrolled here Mr. Browne".

"Brother, what are the requirements here?"

"An eighth-grade diploma, being Catholic, and a ten dollar registration fee."

Getting out his wallet, Browne handed him the money. 'Damn Catholics. It's always about money' he thought to himself.

"Brother, I'd like to see the school," Browne said.

"Certainly. You're free to move about the building."

"One last question, Brother. Are there any native Irish here? I've heard they're great for the discipline."

"There are many. Brother O'Connor teaches history; Brother Hayes, math; Brother Harkins, science; and Brother Murphy, English."

"Brother, thanks. I'll take my tour now and leave for work."

As Browne left the office, he saw a pile of yearbooks in a bookcase. Opening the most recent one, he found a picture of Brother Murphy with a wisp of gray hair covering a balding head. The students, all in ties, were changing classes. One boy crashed into him. "Billy Kelly," an older brother yelled, "watch where you're going, you amadan (fool)."

"Sorry, Brother Murphy. Sorry, Sir." Just the man he was looking for.

With that Browne returned to the subway, pleased that he had located his quarry.

A few weeks later, after having bought a Webley revolver for twenty dollars at a pawnshop in Brooklyn, Browne waited until August to renew his quest. But when he called Rice High School, the receptionist told him that Brother Murphy was on vacation at the seminary in West Park, New York, over three hours from Brooklyn. Borrowing a car from a friend, Browne headed for the place which he found on Road 9W just north of Newburgh.

A white frame house sat on a hill surrounded by manicured lawns and trees. Parking at the foot of a circular driveway, Browne walked toward the building surprised to find a dozen cars ahead of him and a crowd of brothers in black suits walking behind a casket in a funeral procession going to the cemetery nearby.

Frustrated, he drove back to the city. He would try again.

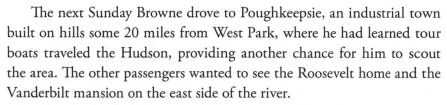

The next Sunday Browne drove to Poughkeepsie, an industrial town built on hills some 20 miles from West Park, where he had learned tour boats traveled the Hudson, providing another chance for him to scout the area. The other passengers wanted to see the Roosevelt home and the Vanderbilt mansion on the east side of the river.

When he finished the ride, he drove again to West Park.

BART MURPHY

SIXTY YEARS LATER IN the sick bay of the Irish Christian Brothers in West Park, New York, eighty miles from New York City, Brother Bart Murphy was fading a little every day from chronic emphysema. In his early eighties and after sixty-two years in the congregation, much of it spent as a teacher and librarian in Harlem, he was tired of that millstone from his youth— shooting Major Browne— that haunted all his nights and days, yearning for the release that only death can bring.

Browne's Quest

While listening to the radio, Browne heard a commercial for the Berlitz language academy, which sparked an idea in him. Usually students attended the school to rid themselves of their Irish brogue. Browne, however, wanted to soften his clipped English accent, a dead giveaway to anyone Irish whose language was guttural. Calling the school, he spoke to a receptionist and explained what he wanted. "Please remain on the phone while I ask one of our instructors."

"Hello, Sir, Mr. Palms, a linguist said he can help. Two months of class three times a week two hours a class."

"What is tuition?"

"$5 a class plus books and materials."

"Fine," Browne said, "When do I start?"

"Monday, Sir, at 6:00 in Room 2416 on the second floor."

CLASS

PALMS WAS A GOOD teacher, first going over the five Irish vowels and then the twelve vocalic sounds. He made Browne mimic the sounds and gave him a tape recorder to listen to the sounds and then repeat them. An ideal student, Browne arrived in class before the professor who was all business, just the way Browne liked it. Some of his work involved learning some Gaelic or "Irish" as the natives called it. To Browne, Gaelic sounded like someone talking with stones in his mouth. Some Irish Americans talked very fast earning the name "turkey birds". After two months, Browne was happy with his improvement. He practiced with his coworkers on the docks who noted how improved his speech was. "No more limey," Jerry Foy said. Browne could even understand some of these Irish bastards.

FLASHBACK

BROWNE THOUGHT BACK TO the beginning of his search for the man who killed his brother. The only man who knew of his plan was the informer Tom Clancy, but would he be alive after more than twenty years? The only way to get at Clancy would be to travel to Dingle though he hated the place. If his enemy wasn't dead, Browne would kill him. He could check if Clancy was there by calling Dingle long distance.

Browne asked the Irish operator for the phone number for Tom Clancy. She replied," The idjit has no phone. All his money goes for Drink. He still lives in town, but with no phone. Sure, we have to get a messenger boy to fetch him when he has a call. Do you wish me to send for him?"

"No, Mrs. that won't be necessary."

Now that Browne knew that Clancy was in place, he would have to find out where Bart Murphy was. West Park was out of the question at least for a while because he was known there. He called Rice High School and asked if Brother Murphy was available. The secretary answered, "No, Sir, he's on sabbatical in Dingle his home." Perfect. They were both in the same place.

PASSPORT

ONE PROBLEM BROWNE HAD was his English passport. He would need one for Ireland. After asking his coworkers at the steel mills for a good forger, he found a name—Abraham Issacson, a tailor, on West 33rd Street in Brooklyn. Because Jewish shop owners were superstitious about making the first sale of the day, Browne would go early just as the man was opening up his store

Nate Issacson the tailor asked, "Is it a suit you're looking for?"

"Not just yet," Browne said, "I need some papers first."

"I see," the tailor said.

Isaacson went to the door and pulled down a closed sign. "Come into the back of the shop." Neatly arranged on a table were a sewing machine, a steam iron, buttons, and scissors. In a locked drawer, the tailor pulled out many passports tied with a rubber band. A black sheet covered a camera in the corner.

"And how do I address the passport?"

"To the United States," Browne said.

"I have plenty of those."

"What name do you wish to use?"

"William Greene with an 'e.'"

"I'll need your age, birthday, and place of birth."

"Fifty-one, London, 1912."

"Fine," said Isaacson, taking out a blank passport. "I'll type in the information and then smudge it to look used. Write your signature at the bottom. Do you have a picture of yourself?"

"No," Greene replied.

"I have a camera here we can use, $75 total," Issacson said. "Expensive, but I've never had one come back to me."

"Fine," Greene said counting out the money.

"Go behind the sheet for the picture." Isaacson took three shots before he found one he liked. He smudged that too. "Well, Mr. Greene, you're now official."

"Our transaction is private."

"Of course, Mr. Greene. Now about that suit. I have a blue serge that would look good on you. I'll measure you right now."

"Good, but I want it by late tomorrow afternoon," Greene said.

"It'll be ready for you."

Browne thought about killing the tailor, but too many of his fellow workers knew he had gone to see him.

Browne was pleased with himself. One part of the job done. He had saved enough money for the flight, now for the reservations.

ST. MARY'S

THE THREE-STORY NOVITIATE BUILDING named St. Mary's housed 15 novices, new recruits, ranging in age from 17 to 25, most from New York but a few from Chicago and Canada where the brothers had schools. Their goal was to become high school teachers and their life consisted of Mass, prayer, and classes in education, philosophy. theology—and sports—baseball, football, hockey, and basketball.

Along with the novices was a group of twenty older brothers retired, or close to it in their 70's, most of them Old Country. The two separate groups came together for Mass and meals, otherwise, their schedules differed. The older men came from a nation which had survived the long siege with England which didn't end until 1948 when Ireland became independent. In World War II Ireland had an official policy of neutrality even though 50,000 Irishmen fought against the Axis powers, and Ireland offered the Donegal corridor for British planes to fly over the country. There was also cooperation between Irish and British intelligence about weather information, including the final decision to launch D-Day based on a weather report from Black Sod Bay in County Mayo.

St. Mary's Novitiate sat in the mid-Hudson Valley on Road 9W between Newburgh and Kingston, three hours from New York City. With the mighty Hudson flowing a quarter mile below the novitiate and both sides of the river enshrouded by hills and trees the area resembled Ireland. In fact an Irish priest, Monsignor Power, working in New York, had discovered the site, bought it from a Rockefeller cousin, envisioning a Catholic college on the grounds, and donated it to the brothers who honored his memory by naming a school for him, Power Memorial Academy.

One difficulty the brothers had was the declining health of its aging members, some of whom needed full-time health care. For years the brothers had managed their own health concerns, transporting the sick to Benedictine Hospital in Kingston to doctors; but as the number of infirm brothers increased, the congregation began to consider full-time nursing care. They didn't do hospital work because the brothers took a vow of celibacy, they interacted very little with women and would have to adjust to female nurses.

In addition to meals together, the brothers lived a community life through which they formed friendships and built camaraderie, often difficult because they had hailed from different parts of Ireland and had taught in different American schools.

Just south of the cemetery the brothers had constructed a farm with two dozen milk cows and a coop for with thirty chickens, in this way supplying much of their own food.

With the suffering resulting from Ireland's protracted war with England, the leadership of the congregation banned all discussion of politics, which was easier said than done. At breakfast one day, Brother Verde asserted "Michael Collins was nothing but a philandering gunman, holed up in a Cork hotel with Kitty Kiernan. He got what was coming to him."

"A black lie," retorted Bart. "What would you know of Michael Collins, you living on an iceberg in Canada?"

"They shot him in his home county. That tells you how the people who knew him best regarded him."

"You fool, he saved Ireland," Bart yelled.

"Brothers, no more politics,'" Brother Wight said. "It only leads to argument."

A WOMAN'S TOUCH

AGNES DUHIG LIKE HER sister came from a small farming and fishing village in Kerry called Ventry about five miles west of from Dingle. The oldest male inherited the farm, so girls had to find work, most often in New York

Mercy nuns and other Catholic nuns founded The Mission of Our Lady of the Rosary for the Protection of Irish Emigrant girls. During the American Civil War, native-born Irish nurses served as 20% of the total of nursing staff. Though she had attended school to grade twelve, she could read and write in both English and Irish and had worked at St. Jude's Hospital in Oak Park near Tralee, a home for retired priests. Though beautiful and strong with ebony hair, she was capable and had a good sense of herself. She came to America and studied in the Mercy school for a month of training.

"Yes," he said, "those mansions on the right are the homes of the wealthy—Roosevelt, Vanderbilt and others. This is the greatest country in the world. It's clean with plenty to eat." Brother Dan was a mumbler with only faint traces of a brogue. "I'm from Dublin, Miss."

"Please call me Agnes, Brother, it's much more informal. What is that river, Brother? We followed it all the way from New York."

"The Hudson. It runs from the sea to the mountains up north. It's three-quarters of a mile wide here."

"Do some of the young men swim across?"

"Yes, but it's dangerous with deep and shifting tides. A brother of one of our young men, Brother Rose, drowned a few years back. When we informed his mother, she died of a heart attack. We live on the west side of the river. On the east side live the robber barons, big shots like Roosevelt and Vanderbilt. Our seminary is small compared to those places."

"I went to school with the Presentations. Sure there was a flock of them. How many brothers are in your seminary?" Agnes asked.

"Eight old fellas like me and about twenty novices or trainees who come and go, some to teach and some who leave the order."

"Brother, are there any other nurses working here?"

"No, you'll be the only one, but I think you'll do well," said Brother Dan. "You have a nice way with you."

From Brother Dan, Agnes learned that the Christian Brothers had been founded in Waterford, Ireland, by Edmund Rice, a merchant who wanted to teach poor boys.

Most of their schools were in New York, but they had others in Chicago, Seattle, and Montana. She had even visited one of their schools in the Bronx, All Hallows, to get a feel for their work. The brothers and staff there received her kindly though they didn't fully understand the purpose of her coming. Agnes would never know the uproar her hiring would cause in the community of men in West Park who taught in all boys' schools.

A BEAUTY

AGNES DUHIG WAS TWENTY-THREE when she left home; and with her dark hair and fair skin dotted with freckles, she was a beauty. She had little experience dealing with men except for her one brother. However, she had a good sense of herself and would play the fool for no man.

The arrival of Agnes Duhig caused a sea change in the seminary. Kind and very conscientious, the only woman in the house, she cared for all her patients. Even Brother Pierce—who didn't like anyone—admired her.

When they arrived at the seminary, St. Mary's, with four floors, the size of the place overwhelmed her. A large frame house sat on top of a hill surrounded by trees and manicured lawns.

The brother in charge was Brother Wight, a stocky ruddy-faced man in his forties. He introduced himself and explained that most of her work would be nursing care for the eight old men. For poor old Brother Lannon who had dementia, she would have to bathe, dress, and clean up after him. "Some of the men may be cross and crabby, but they will come around in time once they realize you're here to help them. As for the young men, the novices, they are here to study and pray. Keep your distance from them because you're attractive and may be a distraction for them. But don't allow any of them to disrespect you."

Agnes blushed, but Brother Wight kept on talking. "Your salary will be $300 a week that includes room and board and one day off a week. Is that satisfactory?"

"Yes, Brother."

"I'll show you to your room which is on the third floor close to the older brothers." The room was clean but spartan containing a bed, a chair, a desk and only religious objects—a large crucifix and a picture of the

Blessed Virgin Mary. Next door was a shower, toilet, and bathtub. "Brother Dan will drive you to a drugstore in Newburgh for any toiletries you need. Bells go off at all hours, but you'll get used to them. This can be a lonely old place for all of us. On your days off, you may wish to take a train to the city. Br. Dan will drive you to the train and pick you up."

"Thanks, Brother, I have cousins there. What about Mass, Brother?"

"Every day at 6:45, but we don't expect you to attend daily. That's up to you. Once you're settled in today, you can meet some of the brothers. Mass is the same time on Sunday."

"One request, Brother," she asked Brother Wight. "Please call me 'Agnes' instead of Miss. It's more informal like."

Agnes attended Mass most days except when she had a sick brother to tend. She wore a shawl to cover her head, the Catholic custom for women in church, showing respect for the Blessed Sacrament. Sitting in the last pew, she observed the piety of the community who answered the prayers in Latin.

"Yes, Agnes. Two worries: Wild dogs are a danger to us up here with so many woods around us, so if you're out for a walk, and hear or see dogs, head back to the house and see Brother Dan. Also, last month a strange incident."

"Good God, what's that all about?"

"We don't know but we've had the sheriff out to investigate. The shooter hasn't been around for weeks, so maybe we're clear of him."

"Brother, living on a farm my whole life, I'm used to dogs, both wild and friendly. And my father taught us to shoot rabbits in the garden, so if you show me where the gun is kept I can fend for myself. If see any strangers, I'll report to you. Also, I have a younger sister at home, Eileen, who is a great shot. If she ever comes here to work, she can be independent."

"I'll keep that in mind," Brother Wight said. "Why don't you tour the place now. No one will bother you. Then later we can meet some of your patients."

Brother Wight thought it might be best to see the crabbiest brother first, so he knocked on the door of Brother Verde, who answered gruffly, "Come in." Brother Wight introduced her as Nurse Agnes Duhig. Suffering from poor circulation in his legs, Brother Verde had a very hard time getting out of bed. Wanting to test her, he asked "Nurse, can you help me out of bed to sit down?" Agnes said, "I think so Brother. I've lifted ten-gallon cans of milk on our farm." She put her arms behind Brother Verde's back and neck and pulled him up to the side of the hospital bed before helping him shuffle to a chair.

"Have a seat, Agnes, so we can talk. William, you can clear out now. We'll be fine. Where are you from?' Brother Verde asked.

"From Ventry on the Irish coast close to Dingle," Agnes said.

"Can you tell me, Agnes, why is Kerry called the 'Kingdom'"?

"Brother, I suppose one reason is that it is so isolated and secluded. Mainly Irish is spoken there. I know it myself. On a map it's like a long bony finger into the Atlantic."

"Agnes, the Irishmen go on and on about the Black and Tans. Who were they, and why did the Irish hate them so?"

"Brother, 'The Tans' as we Irish call them, were not regular army but 'irregulars' who had survived the Great War and needed a job. The worst of them were prisoners and thugs let loose on us, by Churchill and England, sending 10,000 of them here to persecute us. They killed my grandfather coming from Mass in 1921. Finally, they became so notorious that England pulled them out."

"I've learned more from you in five minutes than in all the years I've lived with the Irish."

"Where are you from, Brother?"

"From Nova Scotia, which means New Scotland, a province of Canada."

"Did any more of your countrymen join the brothers?"

"Only one Agnes and he left, so I'm the only one."

"Can I get you some tea or a glass of water?"

"A cup of tea would be wonderful, no milk or sugar, please Agnes."

"I'll be back with your tea in a few minutes, Brother."

When Agnes left the room, Brother Wight approached her to see how she had gotten along with Brother Verde: "I'm getting Brother some tea. We'll be fine."

Agnes walked the two floors to the kitchen where Brother Dan was making dinner. Besides being the house driver, he doubled as cook on a large kitchen stove with four burners and a large refrigerator. When Agnes said she was bringing tea to Brother Verde, Brother Dan said, "Fine, but you can't be running your legs off at every request. The kettle is on the stove, the tea in the cupboard."

Once Agnes brought the tea, she went to the next room, that of Brother Pierce who had a shock of white hair and scurried around his room. "I'm Brother Pierce," he said. "I teach catechism to the young boys and girls in Kingston, still working after sixty-one years, unlike these convalescents."

"But, Brother, some of these men are too sick to work."

"Sure they could if they really wanted to," said Brother Pierce.

"Could I get you a cup of tea?" she asked.

"No, Miss, I can get my own tea without a woman's help."

This was the first rebuff that Agnes received, but she promised herself that it wouldn't deter her from her job.

The next brother she spoke to was Brother Angelus, an Irishman in his seventies who taught the novices math. Close to his chair he had placed a blackthorn stick, an Irish cane of red wood with mean little knobs that helped him get around. The steep stairs were a torture for him. Agnes thought all the old brothers should have a cane.

He was always busy preparing the math classes he taught to the novices and oral reading to Brother Denis from Chicago. An excellent teacher, he told his students to come for help any- time. He loved teaching, no matter the abilities of his pupils. He had been a fine handballer in his youth, but a broken hip had ended his sports career.

Agnes learned that he had been a firebrand for the IRA in his youth, sometimes even hiding guns under the altar cloth. But she would never talk to him about that. He left Ireland because the Irish brothers wanted him away from politics.

Agnes told him she was from Ventry in the southwest of Ireland. "I'm from Limerick," he said, "But I didn't see much of the country, unlike these Yanks who go everywhere."

"You're right, Brother. It's only two hundred miles from West to East, but it was hard to get around. Agnes asked him "Would you care for some tea?'

"I would indeed. Thanks for asking."

The next brother Agnes met was Brother Bart who was interested in her because she was old country from Ventry close to Dingle. "My mother was from Dingle. Perhaps you knew her—Bridie Kevane."

The news stunned Bart. "Oh yes. She was a close friend of my brother Jerry. The last time I saw her we were grieving over his body."

"She told us the story often. Wasn't the Black and Tan leader killed too? He had murdered a priest during the Rising."

"He was a killer who deserved to die, Agnes."

From that time Bart and Agnes became very close. A friend, she was a powerful connection to his past.

Agnes and the Killer

Every afternoon when Agnes had completed her work, just to get out of the house, she went for a stroll on the concrete path called the Rosary walk, close to the cemetery and a bit farther into the woods, always impressed that the brothers, even the novices stopped there to pray—even after their games or apple picking. Agnes followed their example, stopping at the cemetery to pray for her deceased grandfather murdered by Major Browne and the Tans in Tralee. She thought of the difficulty Brother Murphy had while walking, thinking he would do better with a cane.

This was a lovely fall day with the Hudson reflecting the oranges and reds of the trees on the other side of the river.

She was thinking of this when a stranger surprised her by stepping out from bushes behind the cemetery. Dressed in a blue suit, the man was as surprised as she and walked toward the house.

Agnes said to the man, "What are you doing here? This is the property of the brothers."

"I'm here to visit the grave of Brother Murphy," the man said with a strange brogue.

Agnes realized that this might be the man Brother Wight had warned her about. As she scurried toward the house, the man pulled out a Webley revolver and fired a shot at her high and wide because he tripped on the edge of the cement path. Browne would even kill a woman. "Dirty bitch," he yelled as she dashed into the house.

Agnes called for Brother Dan: "There is a man with a gun just outside." Dan grabbed his rifle and went out to face the man. Browne raised his gun. But Dan was too fast for him and shot the man in the shoulder. Dropping his gun, Browne lurched into the woods clutching his left arm and staggering through the trees toward his car, Brother Dan following the trail of blood.

The shooter stumbled through the shrubbery toward the road. He tore down 9W headed for the city. His arm burned, and he was afraid of fainting from the loss of blood.

When Brother Murphy heard of the shooting, he felt guilty. Here was this beautiful Irish girl shot at because of his sin from years before.

BROWNE'S WOUND

HIS SHOULDER STILL BURNING and bleeding from the bullet wound, Browne staggered into the office of Dr. Goldblum who treated all the workers from the Brooklyn steel mills. Because the shot had gone clean through his arm, the doctor had only to disinfect the wounds, sew him up, bandage the wounds on his arm and back, and inject a pint of blood.

"Doctor, can you write me a letter to my supervisor at work excusing me from duties for two weeks?" Browne asked.

The doctor agreed.

The damage to the assassin's psyche was huge. This was the second time he had failed to shoot the bastard brother. How had the devils known he was coming? Was it by pure chance they had caught him out—that some young woman happened to be at the cemetery to summon an armed brother just as he was nearing the house and to shoot him? Browne didn't think so. During his time off work, he would have to plan again.

That was too much coincidence.

BART'S SILENCE

FOR THEIR PART, DAN in West Park called Sheriff Olson in Newburgh to investigate the shooting. Such an incident was rare in this rural atmosphere. When Olson came, he found a Webley revolver in the woods close to the house. The revolver was one which thousands of British used against the Irish in the Anglo-Crown conflict. Browne had purchased his at a pawn shop in Brooklyn.

BAKED SILENCE

FBI

Just to be on the safe side with the shooting, Sheriff Olson reported to the F.B.I. that an unknown assailant, possibly Irish or English, had made an attempt at shooting Brother Murphy, an American citizen. The agency had infiltrated Irish national organizations such as Clann Na nGael (our Irish family) for years, but these groups targeted English, not Americans.

One agent, though, was interested in the report. Sam Catalanotto had an Old Country Irish mother and an Italian father. Having heard stories about the Black and Tans from his mother and uncles all his life, he was determined to follow up on the matter. His supervisors approved his request to investigate especially since foreign nationals might be involved. Also, he was planning a vacation to Ireland with his family later that summer, so he could combine business with pleasure and track the assailant if he was there.

Catalanotto's first step was to interview Brother Murphy, the target of the shooting. He called the brother for an appointment, which made Bart anxious. Would he ever be free of this burden from his youth?

**Mid-Hudson Valley. Note the Vanderbilt Mansion
on the right, a half mile from Esopus.**

Photo by Jack O'Keefe

Admiring the beauty of the river and the Vanderbilt Mansion on the east side of the river where the Secret Service lived. The Catalanotto drove two hours up the Hudson Valley. He found the seminary easily enough and met Brother Murphy in a small parlor on the first floor. Stuffed with holy pictures and statues of the Blessed Virgin and of Christ crowned with thorns, Catalanotto felt he was in a small church. Dressed in a gray suit with a green tie, Catalanotto had a brush haircut with black hair. He presented his F.B.I. credentials to Brother Murphy and explained that he had come to finish the report on the shooting. The brother was ill at ease. To make him more relaxed, Catalanotto mentioned that he was a "brothers' boy" graduating from All Hallows High School in the Bronx, another school run by the Christian brothers.

After shaking hands, Bart started the conversation: "Sure I thought the matter was over. I spoke with Sheriff Olson and your own men. I heard no more about it."

"Just a few questions, Brother. Our report said the gunman may have been a Black and Tan going back to the war with England and he mentioned your name."

Reddening, Brother Murphy replied, "But that's ancient history. That war ended years ago. Why would someone come after an old man after all these years?"

"I don't know but I'm going to find out. Brother, would you show me the scene of the shooting?" Bart walked the agent around the corner of the house to the cemetery and the concrete path leading to it.

"Sheriff Olson found a revolver just on the edge of the woods off the path. Brother Dan fired at him and the blackguard fled through the trees to his car. I never even saw the devil. Mr. Catalannotto, that's all I know. I'm leaving soon for a vacation of one month back to my home in Dingle. You have Olson's report and that from your own men." Remembering his manners, Brother Murphy asked, "Would you like a cup of tea?"

"No thanks, Brother. I have to drive back to New York. Thanks for your time."

The FBI agent found the brief interview disquieting. Having conducted many interrogations during his career, he could sense when someone was lying or holding back. Murphy hadn't told him the full story.

Bart Returns to Rice—Back to School

One strange afterthought. At Rice High School the boy from Brooklyn, the phony son of the Englishman, never enrolled in school.

Bart Murphy didn't know what to do after the shooting incident. He would return to Rice High School in September and resume teaching part-time. All he could do was to keep a sharp eye out for any stranger in case the devil hadn't given up.

HARASSMENT

THE THREE-STORY NOVITIATE HAD stairways at each end. During classes the novices had to use them to get to their rooms or to chapel. They were unfailingly polite when they passed Agnes going to the kitchen. But one brother caused her anxiety. Brother Varrero, the assistant novice master, taught philosophy and Spanish and supervised sports. When Agnes started working at the seminary, Brother Varrero would bump into her on the stairs. At first she thought that this jostling was accidental, but she began to notice it occurred when only the two of them were on the stairs, and with no witnesses. She was being harassed but was in a quandary about what to do. One afternoon was the last straw. Varrero had bumped into her and ran his hands across her breasts. Agnes turned to him and said, "Brother, I've given you no cause to paw me. Stop it." Varrero blushed and said he was sorry. Agnes rarely raised her voice, and one of the novices heard the exchange, spreading the story like wildfire.

When Brother Wight heard about the incident, he was furious, but he had to see if there was any truth to it. Agnes was embarrassed even though she was guiltless. She was only a few weeks working there and wanted no trouble. When Brother Wight called her into his office, she was trembling. "Agnes, I've seen nothing but kindness and hard work from you, but I have to know if any brother has made you uncomfortable."

Tears rolled down her face, and she said, "Brother, I didn't want to bring this up, but Brother Varrero has been touching me inappropriately. I've given him no cause. I feel like a rape victim."

"Agnes," Brother Wight said, "you've been a Godsend to us, and I know your story is true. One of the novices confirmed it. I'll speak to

Brother Varrero and his bad behavior will stop. I'm only sorry it happened. Don't worry about it for a minute more. I'll take care of it."

Brother Wight accused Brother Varrero of harassment.

"Don't you have any respect for your vows?"

"I'm sorry, it won't happen again."

From then on Brother Varrero reformed his ways. He kept his eyes cast downward when he met Agnes on the stairs. The old Irish brothers missed little in their contained environment. At breakfast Bother Verde said, "What can you expect from a dago?" The previous summer while studying Spanish in Mexico, Brother Varrero had harassed several young women. The brothers transferred him to their school in Boston the next year.

BROTHER LANNON

AGNES FELT THE WORST for Brother Lannon, now in his seventies because he had lost control of his bladder and of his faculties and would wander the halls.

Later one afternoon, Brother Pierce came running up to Agnes. "Brother Lannon is urinating on the library books. You've got to do something, or he'll have the whole library destroyed. That's why we hired you."

Agnes spoke to him gently and put him on a schedule of using the bathroom every two hours. She tried to keep him from napping during the day to prevent him from roaming the halls at night.

As Agnes was nearing her first year at St. Mary's, Brother Wight told her "It's time for you to take a vacation."

Agnes replied, "Who will take care of Brother Lannon?"

Touched by her kindness, Brother Wight said, "I should have told you. We've decided to put Brother Lannon in an old folks' home in Kingston." When Agnes started to cry, Brother Wight thought to himself, "This lady is a jewel."

A New Friendship

"Agnes," Murphy said, "You're from Ventry?"

"Yes, Brother, I went to school in Dingle with the Presentations and did much of our family shopping there. My parents and grandparents are buried in Ventry with the cemetery open to the sea."

"Agnes, I would love to make one last trip home if my lungs and my legs were in better form."

"Brother, your breathing and walking are better. You could become stronger by walking every day."

"You're not giving me blarney are you?"

"No, Brother."

———◆◆◆———

So every day Agnes and Bart strolled past the cemetery and Manning's Road, the eventual goal, road 9W, a half mile away. "Brother, my sister Eileen sent me a blackthorn stick for you like the one Brother Angelus uses"

"God bless you."

Shortly afterward Brother Wight called Agnes into his office. "I'm not in trouble, am I, Brother?"

"No, not at all. You have the run of the place. We're all happy to have you—even Brother Pierce though he'd never say it. Agnes, I have two requests. We'd like you to accompany Brother Murphy home. We will pay your airfare both ways and give you your regular salary."

"Oh no, Brother. I've saved my money and can pay for myself."

"Now, Agnes, as you Irish say, 'Look here to me.' You have to assist Brother Murphy on the plane and in Dingle. You both could use a month away and you can visit your family. Brother Murphy will be thrilled. You'll also have to keep an eye out for the man who shot at you. Will that be all right with you?"

"Yes, Brother."

"Another request. You mentioned your sister. Would she be willing to replace you here for the month? You could show her the ropes here first. We'd find her a job at Iona College in New Rochelle when she's finished her time here."

"Brother, Eileen will be ecstatic. She has had the same nurses' training in Ireland that I have."

As Brother Wight had predicted, Bart Murphy was excited by the news, especially that Agnes would be his companion.

Garfinny Bridge, Dingle

Photo by Sharon Loxton
http://www.geograph.ie/photo/912692

BROTHER CARTHAGE

Agnes was puzzled by Brother Carthage, a man in his eighties, who talked to himself on the way to chapel. Noting her interest, one brother explained that Carthage was saying aspirations, short prayers like "Jesus Mercy" or "Mary help me." He may have been remembering Brother Rudolf Cassidy who died of cancer at twenty while a novice under his care.

Agnes knew he came from Connemara and like many Old Country

men loved horses. Agnes went to Brother Wight. "Brother, I noticed a horse farm down the road. Perhaps Brother Carthage might enjoy a trip there."

"A wonderful idea. But see the farmer for permission first."

Agnes visited the farm owned by Tom Mitchell, told him the story, and asked that he might allow Brother Carthage to visit the horses. "Of course," Mitchell said. So one Sunday afternoon, Brother Dan drove Bart, Agnes, and Carthage to the farm. She brought a bag of carrots and sugar cubes as treats. At first, the horses were shy and stood by the fence with Mitchell watching from the barn.

Like all good horsemen, Carthage avoided looking at the horses directly, a sign of aggression, speaking softly to them with the treats in his hand. A black mare was taking most of the treats, so Carthage told Agnes to toss the treats further into the field. That distracted the mare so other horses could share them. Sensing his kindness, the horses allowed Carthage to pet them. When it was time to go, the horses came to the fence sorry to see him go.

Farmer Mitchell came to see the brothers leave. "A real lover horses, I see.

Brother, you may come to visit them whenever you like."

Power Memorial – Death in New York City

St. Patrick's Day in New York is a special celebration for the Irish Christian Brothers with each of their three schools marching in the parade down Fifth Avenue. For years Bart had supervised the marchers from Rice High School which had won many awards. Brother Hendricks, principal of Power Memorial Academy in Hell's Kitchen, phoned West Park to ask Bart if he would help Brother Adams with the Power marchers. Bart was happy to be of some use. Brother Dan drove Bart and Agnes, who was visiting her cousin Mary Jo, to Poughkeepsie for the train to Grand Central.

Mary Jo met the train and they took the subway to Columbus Circle, close to Power and to her home. Mary Jo said "Sure, this area is Hell's Kitchen. A policeman gave it that name years ago when investigating a homicide."

"Sure, 'tis not as bad as Monto back home," Agnes said.

The two cousins went to attend Mass at St. Paul's Church on 60th Street. As they walked along, boys were playing a game with roller skates, wooden sticks, and a rubber disk. "What game is that?" Agnes asked.

"Street hockey. They play it all day until dark. Mind you don't get a puck in the head."

———————

Once they were in church, Agnes said, "Sure, this is as grand as a cathedral. The beautiful ceiling and the stained glass windows."

"Can you imagine that the walls are made of stone from the city's

155

water aqueducts?" Mary Jo said. "The priests got them free. There are no flies on those priests."

Midway through the Mass, firecrackers echoed from somewhere close to them. "What's that?" Mary Jo said.

"Those are gunshots. Sure I heard enough of them in Ireland to know," Agnes replied. "Run on home to Sean and the children. I'll see if I can help anyone." She ran to 61st and Tenth Avenue alongside Power Memorial Academy where a boy leaking blood lay on the sidewalk, a Brother standing over him. "I'm a nurse," Agnes said. "Can I do anything?"

"This boy, Tom Brady, is gone. Just finished Confession. There are some boys at the armory who are wounded. You can help there," the principal Brother Hendricks said.

Tom Brady, Rest in Peace,
March 15, 1948

Agnes ran a block down to the Coliseum where ambulances and police cars flooded the street.

Brother Murphy, who had been helping the marching practice at the armory, stumbled in a daze from the building and met Agnes: "Sure girl, what are you doing here?"

"Trying to help, Brother."

"God bless you, Agnes. This is terrible—several boys wounded. Be careful to stay out of harm's way. The police are still chasing the killer."

Then she met a doctor applying a bandage to a young man. "I'm a nurse, Doctor. Can I help?"

"This boy has a wound in his arm" the doctor answered. "If you could go with him in the ambulance to the hospital, it would be of great assistance."

An orderly loaded the boy into the ambulance for the short ride to Roosevelt Hospital, Agnes kneeling by his side holding his hand.

"I'm Nurse Duhig," she said. "Your arm is hurt, but you will be fine."

"Nurse, how are all the other boys?"

"I'm not sure," she said, not wanting to tell the boy Tom Brady was dead. "What's your name and phone number?"

"Mike Colavito. Hudson 3709."

"I'll dial the number, and you can talk with your mother."

After Mike had finished, Agnes got on the line. "Mrs. Colavito, this is Nurse Duhig from Roosevelt Hospital. Mike has a wound in his shoulder, but he'll be as good as new in a few days."

Agnes stayed with Mike until a nurse from the hospital relieved her. As she was leaving, she bent down and kissed the boy on the forehead.

When she got down to the lobby, police and reporters were milling around. Because her dress was soaked with Mike's blood, Officer Temme drove her back to her cousin's flat on Amsterdam Avenue in a police car.

AFTERMATH

THE CRAZED SHOOTER MARKO L. Markovich, a Croatian immigrant who blamed Catholics for his son's death in a Catholic hospital, left six boys wounded and Tom Brady dead. Police trapped him that afternoon in an apartment building a few blocks away. Bellevue Hospital examined the man after which the court judged him criminally insane and committed him for life to the New York State Mental Hospital in Matteawan, New York. One of the ironies for the brothers was that the hospital was lit up all day and night, visible from the chapel in West Park —reminding them of the man who took Tom Brady's life.

The Parade

More than 1 million spectators and 80,000 parade marchers attended the St. Patrick's parade, as did President Harry S Truman and Gov. Thomas E. Dewey. The celebratory atmosphere of the parade turned somber as the sound of the muffled drums announced the arrival of the Power Memorial Academy contingent at the reviewing stand. The school's principal, Brother William A. Hendricks approached Truman, who expressed his condolences and wishes for those wounded.

"Brother, I'm sorry for your loss, he was a fine young man."

F.B.I. FOLLOW-UP

AGENT CATALANOTTO WENT TO his supervisor Jon Pike for permission to follow up the Murphy incident because the Black and Tans represented a danger to American citizens. The agent would combine business with pleasure, taking a trip with his wife and sons to his mother's home in Ballyferriter, Ireland, less than nine miles from Dingle, to see what he could learn there.

Upon reaching Dingle, his three boys enjoyed the rides in the horse and carriage loaned by a kind farmer inspecting sheep along the road. Catalanotto's, his wife and sons got a ride to Ballyferriter, and the agent was free to work for the day in Dingle.

FBI protocol called for their agents to work with local law enforcement, so as to avoid disagreement with the authorities. Constable LeFevour was the chief law officer in Dingle with an office on Main Street. On the wall hung a crucifix of Christ and a picture of the Blessed Virgin Mary. A statue of Lady Justice holding a balanced scale stood on his desk. Tall and sparse, LeFevour was all business. Catalanotto showed him his credentials, and the constable offered him a chair.

LeFevour began. "You're the first Yank I've seen in a long time and the first FBI man ever. How can I help you?"

"Constable, I'm chasing a story that begins with the Black and Tans if you can believe it. We suspect a former Black and Tan is seeking revenge on Brother Murphy, a Dingle Christian Brother. The man tried to shoot him at the brothers' seminary in New York State."

"Good God," the constable said, "we've been fighting that war for almost thirty years. How does a Yank know about the Black and Tans? Just

163

last year an IRA man shot and killed a Tan in Ballybunion. The ghosts of that war are pursuing us still. Will it ever end?"

"I don't know, Constable, but Brother Murphy told us very little. He's coming here soon with a companion, Nurse Duhig who took care of him in the seminary. I'm here trying to prevent more killing," Catalanotto said. "The man we're after is middle age and English—with a strange accent."

"That's odd, Mr. Catalanotto. Just yesterday I spotted a stranger on Main Street. Because he wore a blue suit, I thought he was a Yank businessman. He may be your quarry. I'll keep a sharp eye out."

"Thanks, Constable. I'm going now to see Brother Hennessy who first warned us about a Tan seeking revenge."

"Mr. Catalanotto, Hennessy will tell a great deal. The hard part is shutting him up. Sure he'd talk the hind legs off a donkey."

HENNESSY

CATALANOTTO WENT TO SPEAK with Brother Hennessy, who had written the warning letter about the informer and Brother Murphy. A big balding man with a voice like all outdoors, Hennessy greeted the agent by saying, "Catalanotto, there's no Irish in that name. There are too many vowels. Are you a dago?"

Long used to racial insults from the Irish, the agent laughed. "My mother is a Rohan from Ballyferriter, my father Italian. Here are my FBI credentials."

Hennessy read the credentials. "What a nice suit you have on, just like those gangster fellas in Chicago." After introductions, Hennessy came to the point right away. "An informer to the Black and Tans, clearing his conscience, told me that a killer had traced Brother Murphy to America and after all these years and wanted to kill him."

"Well, he failed. Another brother wounded the man. I spoke to Brother Murphy in West Park last week. But there is evidence that a man was stalking him."

"Thanks be to God the devil didn't get him."

"Murphy will arrive here next week with a companion, Agnes Duhig, a nurse originally from Ventry. I want to keep them safe," the agent said.

"Brother, tell me who was the informer?"

"Tom Clancy, an old man now. Most days you can find him at The Barefoot Crofter pub on Main Street just down the way. He's overly fond of The Drink, the curse of us Irish."

TOM CLANCY

CATALANNOTTO FOUND THE PUB, peat smoke seeping from under the front door. He felt as if he were walking through a fog. The agent asked the barman, "Is Tom Clancy here?" The bartender pointed to a corner where a slim old man was hunkered down over his drink as if he were afraid someone would snatch it from him. Always wary of strangers, the locals gaped at the man in the suit because he radiated authority, and the Irish had a long history of being suspicious of outsiders.

Catalanotto threaded his way between tables until he came face to face with a wiry man wearing a tweed cap. "May I buy you a drink?" the agent asked.

"You may indeed," replied the older man, "once you tell me what you want. No one buys drinks for nothing."

"Information."

"Well, in that case, order me a double, and we'll move away from so many big ears."

The room was stuffy with the smell of tobacco and of burning peat.

Catalanotto brought back a glass colored with the amber of John Jameson whiskey for Tom Clancy, a froth covered Guinness for himself. Reaching into his wallet, the agent said, "Here are my credentials."

"Put them away. I can tell an honest face when I see one. I know why you're here though it took you long enough to come. I spoke to Hennessy months ago. He wrote the Brothers in America warning them of a Black and Tan assassin who took a shot at him in New York.

"Yes, but much has happened since then, Mr. Clancy."

"Don't call me Mr. Clancy, please. Tom will do."

"The killer worked in Brooklyn and tracked Brother Murphy to West

Park, the seminary, but failed to get him. One of the brothers wounded the man."

"Thank God," said Clancy, "that's one burden from my soul."

"Would you tell me the full story?" Catalanotto asked.

"I will indeed but me throat is a bit parched, like, and it's a story that shames me," Clancy said.

"May I get you another drink?"

"God, yes, this is dry work. A bird doesn't fly on one wing."

Catalanotto rose to replenish their drinks. The fire crackled and spit.

Dropping his voice so low that Catalanotto had to strain to hear him, Clancy said, "I was a secret informer to the Tans. Me mother and little sister Moira were dying of the con ("consumption"—Irish for tuberculosis), and I had no money to pay for a doctor from Tralee. A Tan officer named Percival Browne heard my story from one of his men and bribed me to name the man who made his brother disappear. In the end it didn't matter anyway because Ma and Sis died, God rest their souls. They are now in Garfinney Cemetery, and I gave up my soul to that English bastard. It's haunted my nights and days ever since. Rumor had it that young Bart Murphy, who later joined the Christian Brothers, shot the major in the dead of night and dumped his body into Dingle Bay. I had no proof mind, but it made sense."

"Why?"

The old man took a healthy slug of his whiskey and said, "I keep forgetting that you Yanks don't know our story. Major Browne killed Jerry Murphy, Bart's brother, not two miles from where we're sitting. He shot him in cold blood for being IRA while forcing his brother to look on as a hostage. Bart never forgot it. Even today when he's home, he visits his grave every day."

"Why didn't the army arrest Browne?"

"Sure, you Yanks don't understand the times. The Tans controlled everything. The villagers were so afraid of the Tans that many took to the sea in boats or fled up to the mountains when trouble erupted. Browne went missing, we haven't seen him since."

Catalanotto asked, "Did the rest of the soldiers look for Browne?"

"Yes, but even for them, there was no love lost for the major. A few weeks before, he murdered Father Griffin in Galway, a terrible deed even for the Tans. He made one of his own men, a Catholic, fire the fatal shot. Telling this story has made me thirsty, we being so close to the fire and all."

"Would you like another drink?" Catalanotto asked.

"Yes, the same, please. A bird doesn't fly on one wing."

When the FBI man returned with a Guinness for himself and another double for the old man, Clancy resumed his tale. "I'm glad you're drinking too. Sure the great Michael Collins said 'Never trust a man who don't drink'. Major Browne was a terrible man altogether. He fired on innocent people in Tralee coming from Mass. Then he wrecked the local creamery, destroying milk and butter, starving the locals and depriving them of jobs. Finally, when a French reporter wrote about the siege to the outside world, England stopped it. Then Browne came here after murdering Father Griffin."

"When Browne disappeared in Dingle, the soldiers looked for him?" Catalanotto asked.

"The Tans badgered the whole village, even using torture. They pulled all the fingernails from James Kavanagh, a cousin of the martyr Thomas Ashe, but no one spoke a word—except for me, God help me. When Browne's brother came from Dublin, he was in charge and interrogated us. He had heard the story of my mother and sister and knew of my need for money to pay for a doctor. He bribed me to inform on Bart Murphy, and I told him my suspicions. Later Bart became a religious joining the Christian Brothers in Dublin. Then miracle of miracles, England pulled the Tans out of Ireland because their murdering ways had become notorious the world over."

"What happened to the brother of Major Browne?" Catalanotto asked.

"He went home to England where he got a job in the Birmingham steel mills, and I was happy to be rid of him. But he didn't give up. A few months later, I had a letter from him with fifteen pounds me to track Bart Murphy. Fool that I was, I let him know from the *Kerryman News* that the brothers had transferred Bart to Butte, Montana and then New York. Later I regretted all this because Browne would follow Murphy over the sea to get his revenge. That's the last I heard of him until you walked in here today. I confessed my sins to the priest and told the account to Brother Hennessy, a friend of Bart's who wrote a letter of warning to the American brothers."

"Well, thanks for the information. It will be a great help in hunting this man down."

"This is the last drink I'll ever have. Sure it's time enough for me to stop. I've drunk the River Shannon dry. I'm going take Matt Talbot's pledge to become a pioneer and remain sober till I die. If can help Bart and you, you've only to ask. I live in the last cottage before Garfinny Cemetery."

"Tom, I know that Brother Murphy visits the family grave every day. Could you follow him to make sure he's safe?"

"Gladly," he said. "I'll stay out of sight behind him. I owe it to him and to his family. By the way, never judge those who drink. Matt Talbot, the temperance priest, said, 'Never be too hard on the man who can't give up Drink. It's as hard to give up the Drink as it is to raise the dead to life again. But both are possible and even easy for Our Lord. We have only to depend on Him.' And that's what I'll do—depend on the Lord. So you have no need to fear my informing to Browne again. That's finished."

BART RETURNS TO DINGLE

THE CHRISTIAN BROTHERS ALLOWED each man a sabbatical, a vacation home every seven summers. Bart was especially enthused about the coming summer because the FBI would not be poking into his life in Ireland, as they had in New York, and he would be getting some peace from the pesky Catalanotto. Also, Nurse Agnes would be with him. She was a joy.

The green hills of his homeland cheered him up. Even the screeching of the seagulls in Dingle Bay made him feel at home.

Before he would visit the monastery in town or even go to the cemetery, Bart would see his cousin Deirdre and her husband Ned with their two sons, Tim and George. Bart and Agnes borrowed a horse and carriage from a neighbor and rode the two miles up Spa Road past the Garfinney Bridge and Garfinny Cemetery: "This is where my people are buried," he said to Agnes. Just a glance told him the graveyard was a shamble covered by thick weeds, meadow grass, bracken, and brambles. Cleaning up here was his next order of business.

His young cousin Deirdre lived with her husband Ned and two sons in the original family home, stone newly covered with whitewash and a roof of red corrugated tin. A peat fire burned in the hearth.

A large courtyard of stones with a wooden barn behind it functioned as home for the sheep and dogs. A happy bunch of sheepdogs, white with blue tails, danced around the adults. The largest dog went directly to Bart: "Baron," he said, "you still remember me after all these years. Good dog," patting him on the head and pulling a dog biscuit from his cassock as a treat. Bart recalled his last day when Brother Crimmins shot and killed the wild dogs in West Park.

"This is my nurse Agnes Duhig from Ventry. She's kept me going these last few years."

Deirdre said, "How about a sup of tea and some soda bread? The boys are still out in the fields. You can meet them later."

THE BOER WAR

ON THE WAY TO the cemetery, Bart met an old man, Peter Tullig, his grand uncle. Bart asked, "Uncle Peter is that yourself."

"Barely, Bart. I'm in my nineties and just hanging on." He introduced him to Agnes. "I was so mad at the English that I went to fight them in Africa. Rising martyr Tom Clarke wanted the rebellion to commence during the Boer War in 1910. Yes, after hearing stories from the old ones about The Great Hunger and the landlords, I went to the Boer War and fought the Brits in the Transvaal and the Orange Free State. I killed many limeys but not enough. They murdered the Black Africans by putting them in concentration camps and starving them to death. The devils invented the concentration camps before Hitler."

"What was the fighting like?"

"Terrible in the jungle. In the end, of course, afraid to lose her power, the Brits made alliances with France and Russia, laying the groundwork for the Great War, bastards they are and always have been. Bart, I don't know how much longer I have. Please pray for me."

"I will, Peter."

DEATH

BEFORE BART WENT TO the cemetery, he asked Brother Hennessy if he could cut some flowers to lay on the gravestone. "Take what you like. I'll get you a shears and gloves to cut them. Mind the thorns."

Browne gave a half-crown to a young boy in Dingle to learn where Clancy lived. "On Main Street, Sir, the last house on the right close to the cemetery." Browne would find out if Clancy was the informer and then shoot him. He bought a Webley for twenty pounds at Dick's gun shop on Greene Street. He went to Clancy's house but found no one home.

He decided to take a risk and try the monastery to find Murphy. He asked the Brother at the door if Brother Murphy was in. "No," said Brother Dark. "He's probably at the cemetery." That's where Browne would get his revenge.

When Brother Dark mentioned to Brother Hennessy that a man with a strange accent was asking for Brother Murphy, Hennessy feared it could be the man hunting Bart. "Good God, it could be the Tan after Bart." He then got a horse and buggy to ride to Garfinney, the oldest bridge in Ireland, to check.

Browne found the cemetery easily enough just past the Garfinney bridge. A tall thin cleric with a few wisps of blowing gray hair was kneeling before a gravestone strewn with roses. This would be his revenge. Browne startled the old man from his prayers. "Are you Brother Murphy?"

"Yes. And who are you?"

"Percival Browne whose brother you murdered years ago. What did you do with his body?"

"Pitched it into Dingle Bay. Better than he deserved."

"Do you feel sorry for what you did?"

"Not a bit of it. He was evil. He murdered a priest and my brother."

Pulling the revolver from his coat, Browne said, "Save some prayers for yourself because you're going to die."

Rising from behind the gravestone, where she had been out of sight, Agnes used her hoe to knock the gun from Browne's hand. Reaching to get it back, he yelled "You bitch, I should have killed you in New York when I had the chance. I'll get you now." He shot wildly missing Agnes. He raised the gun and pointed it at Bart when a shot rang out from behind them, spinning Browne around. He crumpled and fell near Jerry's gravestone.

Bart said, "Agnes, please ride the trap to town and fetch Constable LeFevour."

When the constable arrived, he asked, "What happened here?"

Bart answered, "This man Browne tried to shoot me when someone killed him from behind."

"Who?"

"Me," Tom Clancy said walking up carrying a Lee-Enfield rifle. "He was a Black and Tan who chased Bart Murphy for years."

Brother Hennessy came riding up and filled in some of the details. "Browne vowed vengeance on Bart who shot his brother in the Black and Tan wars. He even followed him to America. Well, God knows that we're well rid of the devil before he can do any more harm. He was a killer back to the beginning of the Tans and his brother before him."

Constable LeFevour asked Brother Hennessy to inform Agent Catalanotto in nearby Ballyferriter and bring him back. When the agent came, he was glad—"Browne got what he deserved. Tom, there is a certain justice that you got him." Walking over to Bart, Catalanotto put his arm on Bart's shoulder. "Brother, the devil is dead."

Then Catalanotto went over to Agnes. "You're a hero today."

Agnes's Family

Colm Duhig, Agnes brother, resented her return to America. "You've already taken Eileen away. Who's going to cook and clean house for me?"

"The Lord helps those who helps themselves," Agnes replied. "Why don't you marry?"

"Sure I have no time for courting with this farm on my hands."

"Right down the road is Mary Rooney—a good woman and true."

"She's got a face on her like a pike."

Agnes said, "Have you looked in a mirror recently? All the farmers around us are married. What you want is free labor, to make a slave of one of us. If you're desperate, sell the farm and move to America where there are farms and women."

"It's no use talking to you at all at all."

"And I suppose you think you're Alan the handsome."

BART RECONSIDERS

IN DINGLE BART MET an old friend, Tim Floyd. "Tim, you served in the war?"

"Yes, Bart sad to say I did. Most of my friends considered me a traitor fighting for a neutral country against the Nazis. 12,000 of us."

"God, Tim, I never thought of it that way."

"Many of us died in the fighting. At the end we freed many of the poor souls in the concentration camps. We came home to find no jobs and hatred from our own people. The government has promised to give us amnesty in the future. Can you believe it?"

"Tim, as I say I never thought it would come to this."

"I was blessed to find work on my brother's farm. This was all De Valera's doing. Sure, he even sent condolences to Germany after Hitler's death."

"Tim, I'm sorry this happened to you. I'll pray for you."

Bart's Sin

WITH HIS ASSASSIN KILLED, Bart was ready to return to America, but Agnes found him depressed. "Brother, she said I thought you'd be happy now the devil's dead."

"I should be, Agnes, but I have a wound in my soul that needs healing. I've never told this story to a soul, but I trust you and can tell you my sin. When I was fourteen, I murdered a Tan for shooting my brother. I've never been able to confess my sin after all these years either here or in America."

"Brother, that was war. Surely the Lord forgives you this. You must forgive yourself. You owe it to yourself."

"Agnes, you're right. When we return to West Park, I'll confess and clear my conscience."

FREE AT LAST

ALONG THE HUDSON RELIGIOUS orders had established seminaries: the Jesuits, De La Salles, the Marists, the Redemptorists, and the Blessed Sacrament fathers, and the Cabrini sisters. Because Bart was old country, Brother Wight— following the advice of Brother Angelus—was looking for an Irish priest to administer Extreme Unction, the sacrament of the dying, to Bart. After many phone calls, he finally found one. Father Ignatius Smyth had been a Blessed Sacrament father for fifty years. Brother Wight got him on the phone. He asked "Father, could you come over and administer the last rites to an old Irish brother and hear his confession. He doesn't have long and he's very anxious. We would pick you up and drive you back."

"Certainly, I'm too old to do much around here. I would love to help, and I speak Irish."

"Wonderful, Father. Give me a day and time."

"Tomorrow at noon, Brother. That should give us enough time."

The next day Brother Wight drove over the Poughkeepsie Bridge past the Roosevelt and Vanderbilt estates to the Blessed Sacrament seminary.

Father Smyth came from the building carrying a briefcase with the holy oils for anointing the sick and dying. Tall and with a shock of white hair, the priest was friendly and talkative with Brother Wight.

When they reached St. Mary's, Brother Wight walked the priest to Bart's room.

"An bhfuil Béarla agat? "Do you speak Irish? asked Bart.

"Tuigim" Father Smyth said. "I do"

Both men were from Kerry and conversed easily with each other.

When Bart grew tired, Father Smyth asked, "Would you like to confess now Brother?"

"Yes."

"Go ahead, Brother."

"Bless me, father, for I have sinned. When I was a young man, I murdered a Tan by shooting him in the chest for killing my brother. Since then I've made hundreds of bad confessions. Will the Lord ever forgive me?"

"He already has, Brother."

"Out of pure devilment, I went to Hyde Park and made water on Roosevelt's grave."

Father Smyth laughed. "I wish I had done the same."

Bart giggled.

"Brother, I'm going to absolve you now, give you the Eucharist for Extreme Unction, and together we'll say a decade of the rosary for penance.

"Father, will you be my friend and come and see me once before I go?"

"Yes, I will.

"Brother, I didn't tell you my story. When I was nine, the Tans killed my father coming out of a church in Tralee on All Saints Day. I hated the Tans for years until I read "Easter 1916" by Yeats, where he writes 'Too long a sacrifice can make a stone of the heart.' In my own life, I knew that I had to lift the stone from my heart. We've both suffered. It's time we're at peace." He blessed Bart again.

Driving Father Smyth home, Brother Wight asked, "How did it go, Father?"

"A good and holy man is at peace."

"Can I pay you, Father?"

"Oh no. This has lifted up my soul."

———◇◈◇———

A few days later Bart slipped away in the presence of Father Smyth and Agnes who held his hand throughout. The brothers held his wake in the West Park chapel and buried him in a plot not two miles away from his nemesis, F.D.R.

It was a warm sun-filled day in the Hudson Valley. White gravestones filled the brothers' cemetery, encircled by pine trees laden with chattering cardinals.

Brother Wight, Bart's superior at Rice and in West Park, gave the eulogy to a crowd of a hundred people, some brothers and former students from Rice:

"Brother Bart Murphy labored in the Lord's vineyard for sixty-four years. In addition to his kindness and dedication to his students, he bore an unusual burden: As a fourteen-year-old boy in Dingle, he was hostage to the Black and Tans who were going to shoot his brother Jerry. Only a few feet away, he witnessed the death of his brother Jerry. As we humans do, Bart wrapped himself in guilt, assuming the blame for his brother's death. In Ireland on sabbatical, Bart visited his grave daily, his way of never forgetting Jerry's sacrifice. At the end of his life, Bart wanted only to make a good Confession. Father Smyth of the Blessed Sacrament Fathers across the river told me that Bart died a good and holy man. His nurse Agnes Duhig risked her life for him. May we all be so blessed."

Jack O'Keefe at Ballyristeen, County Kerry, Ireland 2010

REVIEWS

FRANK WEST: *IRISH AMERICAN News*—O'Keefe's previous novel, *Brother Sleeper Agent: The Plot to Kill FDR*, is a riveting, compelling mystery of the IRA's attempt to kill FDR.

Review excerpts:

"O'Keefe is a champion at telling this well-crafted tale of life in Dingle, Ireland, and the rough Irish community of New York in the 1930's and 40's. O'Keefe's wit, skill and pacing keep the plot flowing, as the richly developed characters, and their internal struggles are brought to life in this suspenseful story."

Helen Gallagher, *Release Your Writing*

"About *Survivors of the Great Irish Famine,* O'Keefe makes the story come alive by using a vigorous and memorable storyline. He develops the story with fictional characters but constantly with The Great Famine as the background." Frank West, *Irish Books and Plays in Review. Irish American News.* October 2011.

"Although his parents emigrated from Ireland, they never talked about the Famine or the Easter Rising and its devastating effects on their ancestors." O'Keefe has since" written two books that capture the reality of the time while providing readers with vivid tales of heroism, pride and vengeance."

Caroline Connors, *Beverly News*

Printed in the United States
By Bookmasters